Valor moved further into the shadows of the closet, shrinking back and pulling her knees close to her chin. She held her knees to stay her feet from moving out of the storage room. Her mind was filled with visions of tearing at Kirk's throat with her bare hands and of using the butt of Jed's rifle to pound that red beard into the dust of the sideyard.

As she looked out of her hiding place, she could see Ben's body lying on the porch. Her rage turned to a sorrow that threatened to choke her. Then the rage tore at her again. She held on to her knees. Through clenched teeth, she whispered, "I will hurt you. I will. For what you did to my mama and to Ben. I'll hurt you. Just wait and see, Colonel Kirk!"

GLORIA HOUSTON
Mountain Valor

ILLUSTRATIONS BY
THOMAS B. ALLEN

The Putnam & Grosset Group

Library of Congress Cataloging-in-Publication Data
Houston, Gloria. Mountain Valor / Gloria Houston.   p.   cm.
Summary: With her father and brothers gone to serve in the Civil War
and her Mother sick, thirteen-year-old Valor ignores what is proper
behavior for a girl, and takes matters into her own hands and dresses
as a boy to avenge a wrongdoing and defend her North Carolina family.
1. United States—History—Civil War, 1861–1865—Juvenile fiction.
[1. United States—History—Civil War, 1861–1865—Fiction.
2. Sex role—Fiction.] I. Title. PZ7.H8184Mo   1994   [Fic]—dc20
92-26218 CIP AC
ISBN 0-698-11383-7

10   9   8   7   6   5   4

Dedicated to my wonderful daughter,
JULIE ANN McLENDON,
who taught me that
"Courage is not lack of fear. Courage is feeling
the great fear, and doing a thing because it must be done"
when she wore wings and her "run-fast shoes."

With special thanks to: Frank Vance, a dear cousin, for suggesting that I write this story;

Mil Searls, for computer work on endless revisions and for terrific advice;

Paula Wiseman, my editor, for patience through endless revisions, ten years of research, and superb advice;

Dennis Woody, for information about the English farm on the North Toe River, which was a stop on the Underground Railroad;

Walton Rawls, for his expertise on the Civil War;

and to the craftsmen, especially the blacksmiths and gunsmiths, at the Ozark Folk Life Museum, Arkansas.

And thanks also to: John Parrish, columnist, "Roamin' the Mountains," *The Asheville Citizen-Times*, for information about Melinda "Sam" and Keith Blaylock; the Appalachian Room of Maryland Community College, Spruce Pine, North Carolina; and Ruth Greene Houston, for her knowledge of herbs and their medicinal uses.

CHAPTER 1
(1861)

The cannons' fire on the battery of Fort Sumter had served as a call-to-arms for timbermen cutting in the hardwood forests and farmers tilling the rich black soil of the hills and hollows of the Appalachian Mountains. Some heard on the April air the call-to-arms from the South, while others responded to the answering voice of the North. Early crops rotted in the fertile fields, untended as fathers, sons, and brothers echoed each battle cry and rode away to face one another on barren fields, where some would rest forever in the red clay soil of Georgia or the heavy loam of Pennsylvania, in fields so far away from the steep mountain earth they loved.

But as the summer wore on in the first year of a war, which pitted mountain men against their neighbors and ripped close kin families apart, letters arrived at the mountain farms, homesick letters, lonely letters, but always letters assuring wives and sweethearts that whichever side the writer was fighting for would win, letters filled with hope that the farmers and timbermen would be home in time to cut the fodder and to stack the last of the summer's hay. Wives and sweethearts read the letters and believed the truth in them as the summer twilight pushed shadows in the shapes of towering mountains across meadows waving midsummer green sprinkled with gold.

The shadows crept ever closer to the house John McAimee had built for his pretty Sarah. The whitewashed house with a shake roof glowed against the green of the northern end of a meadow so high that on this clear evening Sarah could see across the Appalachians all the way from the jagged cliffs of Grandfather Mountain to the somber black ridges of Mount Mitchell.

As darkness spread over the valley, the last rays of sunlight turned the sky to lavender, rose, and orange. From the creek bed, tree frogs sang a message that first frost was only a few weeks away. Their song grounded the melody of a lonely fiddle, played by a bent man with a halo of white hair crowning his warm brown face, and the staccato click of a limberjack's feet as a small girl danced, gliding the tiny movable man carved from hickory wood out over the edge of the porch and back again.

Valor McAimee's heart danced with her limberjack and her blue eyes sparkled as she skipped across the porch steps, for only that day a letter had come from her papa saying that he would be home from the war before the new baby arrived. Each time Ben played the chorus of her papa's favorite song, she danced with her limberjack. With the words, "He whistled and sang 'til the green wood rang, and he won the heart of a lady," the small girl's hoop skirts swayed, and she leaped high into the air, making her brown curls bounce.

"Miss Vallie, honey. You about to fall off'n them steps," said a tall woman the color of ebony who sat in one of the two chairs rocking in the corner. In the second chair sat a tiny blond woman for whom she had cared since Sarah was a baby. With little heed of the warning, Valor continued to skip and sing.

"Miss Vallie, take care. Do you hear me?" said the woman. "You be nigh onto ten years old. It's high time you acted like a lady."

"Oh, Savannah. I'll take care," said the child, continuing to skip. "Isn't it wonderful that Papa will be home for the new baby? Isn't it wonderful, Mama?" Valor accented each word with a hop, making the limberjack's feet match hers on the edge of the porch.

"Don't reckon we'll ever teach that one to be a lady," repeated Savannah, continuing to rock as she shelled peas. She passed a handful of pea pods to Valor's mother.

"Yes, it's wonderful, my Vallie," said Sarah. "But Savannah is right. Come away from the steps. You might fall off the porch."

Valor stopped in front of her mother and placed her limberjack's strings over the arm of the chair. She held out her hands and bowed from the waist.

"Miss Sarah, may I have this dance?" she said, making her voice low and gruff like Papa's.

Valor could usually take her mother away from her chores by inviting her to play or to dance. When Valor's older brothers were children, John McAimee had often smiled watching his wife become a child herself as she joined them in their games. Before the boys left for the army, her brothers had made Valor promise to make their mother laugh and dance as she had done with them.

Every day, Valor tried to think of ways to keep her mother from looking so sad when she remembered that Tom and Papa were away fighting for the Confederate States of America. And she tried never to mention her older brother's name or her Uncle Joe's. That made Mama look even more forlorn because it reminded them all that the family was divided by this awful war. While Papa and Tom fought for the South, Jeff and Uncle Joe fought for the North. In Papa's last letter, he had written of the victory at Manassas, but Valor had heard Miss Sarah speak sadly of her only brother's letter of defeat in the same battle.

Valor tried to figure it all out, but thinking about it only made her head hurt. She asked Savannah to tell her about the war and she asked if her brothers were fighting each other by wrestling in the yard, as they did when they were home.

"No, honey," said Savannah, taking the child on her broad lap. "They be fighting each other with guns and bullets, but I reckon old Savannah can't be clear just why they fighting."

It frightened Valor to think of her brothers fighting with guns, but she knew her father would be all right. After all, he had already won a medal for valor fighting on the frontier, so Valor knew he was a very brave man. She hoped her brothers were brave men, too, so they could come home safely, wearing their medals proudly.

"Miss Vallie," said Savannah, "your mama can't dance now. She be too near her time. That baby just about ready to come. We don't want to do nothing to bring it on before Master John get home." She punctuated each word by stripping a pea pod with her thumb.

Valor clapped her hands. She could hardly wait for the new baby to arrive. At last, she would have a playmate. Even before the war, her brothers had been much too old to play with her.

"Please, Mama," said Valor, ignoring Savannah's warning.

Sarah placed her basket of peas on the stool beside her chair and pulled herself up to a standing position, her dress and apron straining against the weight of her pregnancy.

"Vallie, will you stop jumping? Yes, we will dance," said Sarah, her blue eyes looking into two smaller ones just like her own.

Ben stopped playing, poised to help the woman he loved like his own daughter. When he saw that Sarah was safe, he smiled, his warm brown face, the color of coffee with rich cream, haloed with a ruff of white hair. He nodded and sawed away on his fiddle, his melody changing to a soft waltz.

"Miss Sarah," commanded Savannah, "you got no call to be up dancing when you all ready to deliver. If'n I let you hurt yourself, Master John gonna skin me alive."

Sarah smiled. She knew that John McAimee

would never skin anyone alive, least of all the woman who was so much a part of their family that none of them could remember life without her.

Sarah took Valor's hands and began to sing,

"Early one morning just as the sun was rising,
I heard a maiden singing in the valley below;
Oh, don't deceive me; oh, never leave me;
How could you treat a poor maiden so?"

The two danced slowly back and forth. As their song ended, Sarah kissed her daughter, who at almost ten years was only a few inches shorter than Sarah herself.

The valley had grown dark, although the sky was still light overhead. Sarah leaned back against one of the pillars supporting the porch and took a deep breath. Ben stood his precious fiddle against the side of the stone steps.

"I'd better go fasten up the livestock. I left them grazing down by the woods," he said. "No telling when some of them soldiers may ride through here."

"Yes," said Savannah, clicking her tongue. "Like the marauders who raided the poor souls down at Elsie. I hear tell they done stole every animal they had on the place. Hadn't been for the neighbors to help, they'd all have starved."

"Savannah, we ain't seen a soul up this way in nigh onto a fortnight. We some safe here, off the main road," said Ben.

Savannah sniffed. "Ain't no way of knowing when they come. Without livestock, we'd all starve this winter. And we done promised Master John we see to this place 'til he be home again. Now, go along, Ben."

"I'm going. I'm going," said Ben, "as fast as this lame leg will carry me." He limped through the gate in the stone wall.

Savannah rose to her full height, her gray kerchief almost touching the ceiling of the porch as she dropped the pea shells from her apron into the basket. Valor reached over and grabbed a handful of peas. As she began popping peas into her mouth one by one, Savannah slapped the child's hand gently.

"Come on, get out of there," she said, picking up the basket and walking down the front hall toward the summer kitchen. "These be for noonday dinner the morrow. You done had supper."

Valor ate the last of the peas she had taken and reached for her mother's hand. "Let's dance again," she said.

But her mother looked pale. "Vallie, I think you should get Savannah. I think the baby's coming. Help me . . ." her mother whispered.

Valor moved toward her mother. Sarah's face glistened. She was panting and her breath came in gasps.

"Mama," Valor said, "what . . ."

But Ben's voice interrupted. "Miss Sarah," he shouted. "They's Yankees riding up the east slope!"

He limped into the yard. "I'm taking the livestock further back into the woods. You stay hid until I get back."

Valor's eyes widened and she felt her throat grow dry. "Mama," she said.

"Vallie." Her mother struggled. "Help me . . ."

Savannah came charging through the doorway. "Be they gray or be they blue?" she asked, seeming to ignore Sarah's distress. Valor felt herself being scooped into the tall woman's arms. Over Savannah's shoulder, she could see her mother walking slowly behind them, her body rigid, her face pale. "Into the linen press," her mother said faintly.

Savannah set the child down in the front hall that ran the length of the house as Sarah reached her, and opened the door to the storage area under the stairs, quickly removing a stack of rags from a shelf and pulling the shelf out to lay it on the floor.

"Climb in here, Vallie," whispered Sarah, desperation forcing her voice. "Be brave. You have to hide in here until these men leave."

"I'm afraid, Mama," whispered the child, throwing her arms around her mother. "I want to stay with you and Savannah. I'll be brave. I promise. Please, Mama . . ."

Her mother steadied herself against the door. "Honey, remember. We fixed this special place for you to hide," said Sarah. Valor's heart pounded as she looked up at her mother's face, now the color of winter milk.

"Vallie, honey, do you remember what Papa said when he went away?" Sarah smoothed the child's brown braids and smiled weakly. She spoke slowly and deliberately. "He told you, 'Always remember your name.' He even pinned the medal he won for valor on the frontier here on the wall for you. There it is. Remember, he said, 'If you hold it you will always be brave.' Valor means *courage.*" She stopped and took a deep breath. Valor's shoulder hurt where her mother's hand squeezed her. "Please, honey, please remember."

Horsemen were coming through the barnyard, riding single file. Savannah stood in the doorway.

"I remember, Mama," said the child. She glanced toward the door and saw horses filing through the small gateway in the stone wall and into the front yard. Her heart began to pound as she saw the blue uniforms. There was no time to waste. She

18

turned and climbed through the shelf opening and into the closet behind. She pulled the shiny medal with the faded red ribbon from its pin in the wall and held it tightly in one small fist.

"There's a chamber pot in there, a straw tick and some water. You must stay until the men leave. Don't say a word. *Not a sound.* Do you have courage, my little one?" her mother asked. Valor looked at her mother who was clinging to the door frame, her face glistening with fear and fatigue as Savannah replaced the shelf and pushed the door toward the wall, leaving a small opening for light.

"I will have courage, Mama," Valor whispered. "I promise." She crept as close to the back corner as she could and huddled against the wall.

Sarah stepped from the hallway to the porch as the men reached the porch steps. Savannah stood beside Sarah. "What do you want?" said Sarah to the horsemen, her hands clenched in pain behind her back.

"Well, now, pretty lady," said a man taller than the others as he tipped his blue hat slightly. His bright red beard outlined his square chin. "Looks like you are just about to hatch, but you be a mighty fine looking woman." His long legs lifted him from the stirrups and he stood on the porch, his hat touching the rafters. Through the crack in the door,

19

Valor could see a long white silk sash with the letters "HGK" embroidered in red on it, tied loosely around his waist. She read the letters again as he stepped toward her mother.

"Kirk!" whispered Sarah, speaking the name both hated and feared by many throughout the mountains, the name of the man whose troops had burned, stolen, and destroyed homes and farms wherever they marched, leaving the inhabitants homeless and starving. "Oh, God. Help us."

"Colonel Kirk, at your service, ma'am," the man said, smiling down at her and licking his upper lip. "Why don't you come on upstairs with me while your wench here fixes up something for my men to eat."

He took Sarah's arm and pushed her toward the hallway. Valor sat terrified, her back pressed firmly against the wall, clutching her papa's medal to her chest.

Peeking between the shelves, Valor could see the red-bearded man as he pushed her mother roughly up the stairs. She moved toward the opening to see her mother grasp the rail and turn to face the man, who pushed her toward the landing. Reaching out to balance herself, she grabbed at his sash. The silk slipped into Sarah's hands as she fainted and tumbled down the stairs to the hallway floor.

"Mama!" screamed Valor as Savannah and Ben ran to her mother's side. The girl bit her hand as she moved farther into the dark corner of the linen press. The man looked around. "What was that?" he asked.

"It was my old mouth," Valor heard Savannah say from the doorway. "I done screamed out. Miz Sarah here, she just like a mama to us poor folks."

Valor sat inside the dark closet, trying to still her trembling body.

"Well, she's no good to me now," said the man, turning away from Sarah toward the front door. "Might as well see what we can find to eat, if this here Reb farm has any food." He walked out the door. "Let's check out the smokehouse, men," he said as he turned back to Savannah. "You, wench, get to the kitchen. My men need something to eat."

"You see to Miz Sarah. I'll go," Savannah said to Ben.

Valor watched as Ben knelt to lift her mother and carry her into the parlor. She could see the silk sash, now soiled in a trail of blood on the parlor rug, as she sat silently, not daring to move. Frozen with fear, she sat until she heard hoofbeats disappearing into the night. Finally, she peeked out between the shelves and watched Savannah wrap a small bundle

21

in rags and hurry out into the darkness, closely followed by Ben.

"Savannah, Ben," Valor called, "let me out. I want my mama."

But no one heard. It seemed that hours had passed when they finally returned. Savannah opened the closet door wider to look inside. "I done forgot this poor child," she said, moving the shelves and helping Valor climb out of the closet. "Miss Vallie, come on out now."

"Where is Mama?" she said. "I want Mama."

"Your mama be asleep," said Savannah. "Come on, Miss Vallie. Old Savannah sing you to sleep. And we hope you forget all about what you done seen here this day."

"I'm afraid. When is Papa coming home?" asked Valor.

"When this old war be over and when these brothers quit fighting one another," said Savannah. "Oh, Lordy. Make that day come soon."

"Did that man hurt Mama? I hate him," Valor said as she slid off Savannah's lap and stamped her foot. "I hate that mean old man who hurt my mama."

"Honey, we have to let your mama sleep," said Savannah, catching the child's apron and lifting her high in the air to keep her from entering the parlor.

"She hurt some bad. You, me, and Ben, we take good care of your mama. And we take good care of each other until this sad war be over."

"I hate that awful man," said Valor again. "I'll hurt that awful man. I'll hurt him, Savannah, for hurting my mama."

The child pounded the woman's broad shoulder, Papa's medal catching the lamplight as it arced by the gray kerchief tied on the woman's head.

"Be brave, Miss Vallie," said Savannah, smoothing the child's curls.

"I was brave," Valor cried, clutching her papa's medal as she buried her head in Savannah's shoulder.

"Shhh, honey. You did be very brave," whispered Savannah, comforting the child. "Best we forget this night. Shhh."

CHAPTER 2
(1862)

The remains of snow from the first winter of the war that divided the North and the South outlined the rocks in the pasture on the hill farm and clung stubbornly to the rhododendron bushes on the northerly hillsides, despite clear days filled with bright sunlight dawn to dusk. A letter from Papa had told of a terrible battle at a place called Shiloh, and of his concern for adequate supplies for his men. But on the hill farm, the concern focused on making the stored food and firewood stretch into spring and a new summer's harvest. The woodpile Ben and Valor's cousin, Jed, had cut and carefully stacked by the woodshed just after Jed had come to live with them had dwindled to one small row by the south wall near the henhouse.

Ben's ax rang out against the silence, broken only by the skurr of the saw as Jed pulled back and forth.

Occasionally from the distance came the soft cling-clang of a cowbell. The first green shoots pushed through the thick brown thatch of dead grass and oak leaves, so the milk cows had been turned out to graze. Supplies of hay and dried corn were almost gone, drained like the woodpile, by the long cold days and by ground frozen with snow. Grazing the cows would help extend the winter supply in case of a late freeze, which could happen in the high meadow well into May.

Valor's arms ached as she carried load after load of wood into the house. Each room in the McAimee house was heated by a fireplace, and although fires were banked during the daylight hours in every room except her mother's and in the winter kitchen, carrying firewood to supply the household was a constant, boring winter chore. Sometimes Ben would let Valor use the saw, but he would not allow her to touch the ax.

"Man's work," he insisted. "You might maim yourself, Missy. You be only ten year old. Your pa not be liking it if'n Little Missy be hurt when Old Ben not see to her."

Valor stamped her feet as she made her way through the mud to the back door. "Man's work!" she snorted. "I'm as strong as Jed and half a head taller."

Valor threw the wood into a pile in the chimney corner and stamped back around to the front yard gate. Hoofbeats in the distance sounded against the flints in the barnyard road.

Valor's heart almost stopped with fear until the figure grew closer. Sitting astride a tall gray stallion sat the smallest person Valor had ever seen, so small, in fact, that she wondered if she might be seeing one of the fairy folk who brought good fortune in the old stories Mama liked to tell her. She could see that the tiny person wore no hat. Instead, long white hair streamed back in the wind.

The tiny person guided the big horse up to the dooryard gate and reined him in. Valor looked up into a face as wrinkled as a dried apple with wide clear eyes as blue as the winter skies looking calmly back at her. The face was old, but it was one of the more beautiful Valor had ever seen. It was surrounded by a nimbus of white hair shining in the bright sunlight. Valor stood transfixed, staring up at the figure. With a turn of the head the long white hair swung around to cover one shoulder like a ripple of snow. Valor could see the white hair gathered into a topknot, from which it hung down like a horse's tail. Woven into the topknot was a wreath of strange white flowers. A cape of fabric as soft and gossamer as a spider's web, the color of pokeberries in the early summer, covered the body except for one tiny boot of soft black leather. The figure reached to lift a sack thrown across the back of the saddle.

"You! You are a woman!" Valor gasped. "And you ride astride! Who lets you do that?" Valor had never seen a grown woman ride astride. *She* rode astride when no one could see her, but as far as Mama and Savannah knew she rode sidesaddle—like a lady.

"But women . . ." Valor was sputtering with embarrassment and with delight. Here was a woman who rode as she pleased, and who did not care if she rode like a lady or not. Valor laughed out loud. The old woman's face warmed in a smile. The eyes sparkled with merriment.

"I see you be a kindred spirit, my little one," the woman said, her voice soft and gentle like wind soughing through the pines. "We who be sisters to the wind."

Her speech was the language of the old people Valor had heard talking at church gatherings before the war started. It sounded strange to Valor's ears.

"Sisters to the wind?" Valor asked, shading her eyes from the sun that streamed through the old woman's hair.

"Old Estatoe wise-woman lived here after the

rest of her people jined the Cherokee. She used to say that women who was sisters to the wind ken things other mortals do not know. What be your name, Little One?"

"Valor. Valor McAimee," the girl replied.

"Valor. John and Sarah's baby girl." The old woman chuckled. "Born about the time your pa won that medal for valor. Right good choice of a name fer a feisty girl, I reckon. How be your ma doing these days?"

"About the same. Some days, tolerable well. Some not," said Valor. "Did you come to see her?"

"No, I come to bring her some sleeping yarbs and some new-growth birch bark for tea." She lifted the bag down and placed it in Valor's hands as she pushed back her cape and swung one tiny boot over the saddle horn. Then she stepped to the top of the stone wall. As she sat down on the edge of the wall, she draped the reins over her arm.

Valor stared at britches and a short jacket of the same soft pokeberry color as the cape. "You wear britches?" she asked.

The old woman laughed again. "Little Sister," she said softly, "I have the old wisdom, handed down from my mother and her mother before her, brought from distant lands far over the sea. So I'm different. Being different gives a body a freedom

29

most folks never know, even the freedom to wear britches if I've a mind to."

"I'd like to have that freedom," said Valor. She leaned closer to the old lady. "But aren't you fearful of getting into trouble?" she asked.

"Fearful?" said the lady. "I dursen't be fearful of so small a thing. Save your fear, and your courage, too, for the mighty things in life."

"Fear? Courage? The mighty things?" asked Valor, her mind spinning with new thoughts.

"Save your fears, your courage too. Save them for the mighty things. Fear will drive you. So make sure the thing is worth fearing, then courage will grow out of fear," said the old lady, looking intently down at the girl.

The old woman sat silently for a long moment. Then she leaned over, speaking slowly and with great deliberation. "My little one," she said, pushing back the curls from Valor's forehead, "courage is not lack of fear. No, indeed. Courage is being fearful, even being in terror. But courage is being afraid, and doing a thing anyway—doing it because it must be done. You will understand that fully one day."

The old woman seemed to be staring at something in the far distance beyond Valor's face, even as she looked into the girl's eyes.

"Yes, my little one," the woman continued, "I can see that you have great courage, great valor because you are different. You may even be one of us."

"I am different," said Valor, eager to please this remarkable woman. "When nobody's about, I don't ride sidesaddle. I wear my pa's britches sometimes, and sometimes I ride like the wind. Maybe I am a sister to the wind too." Somehow she wanted to be a sister to the wind, to be like this lady.

"Being a sister to the wind gives great freedom, but living different comes with a price, Little One. Most folks see being different as a bad thing to be." The old woman sighed. "Most folks hereabouts believe me to be a witch-woman."

Valor took a step back. Then she remembered the stories Savannah and Ben told sitting by the fire, stories about the witch-woman who lived up Plum-tree Creek near the foot of the Big Yellow Mountain.

Valor remembered riding past the old witch-woman's house in Papa's wagon the summer the war started. "Old witch-woman live there," Savannah had whispered to Jed and Valor that day. "She cast spells and they say she evil, but she know what yarbs make a body well even when you has the pneumony-fever."

"She's not a witch." Papa had laughed at Savannah. "Some say she's a pretty good doctor, Savannah. I like to call her a wise-woman, not a witch."

"Yes, sir." Savannah had lifted her chin and squared her shoulders. "Miz Sarah do swear by that yarb tea Old Auntie mix up for her. And she do sleep better since she been drinking it every night."

"Known her all my life," said Papa. "She's a good woman. Strange, maybe, but a kinder soul never lived."

"Then she don't turn herself into a cat at night?" asked Savannah as the wagon jolted from side to side. Valor had grabbed on to the side of the wagon and looked at Jed with wide eyes.

"No." Papa had laughed. "Stories got started when Aunt Becky was a young woman about how she cast a spell on one of the Charles boys up the road. My uncle Levi used to tell us that she was so beautiful that she made all the men around here fall in love with her. But they say she kept the Charles boy spellbound for the rest of his life. Since he died, she has lived right here in this house he built for her."

"She be mighty old," said Savannah.

"About eighty years," said Papa. "But a kind soul. Always the one to call on if you have trouble. Always ready to lend a helping hand."

Valor looked to the woman who now stood in front of her.

"Are you a witch-woman, Auntie?" asked Valor, holding her breath, her eyes wide, returning her mind to the present.

"Depends on how you think of a witch, I reckon," answered the old woman. "I knows more about how folks thinks and what makes them behave in ways more'n some. I knows more about plants and yarbs to make folks sick or well than some. I have lived longer than most folks, so I have learned a lot from just living. My ma was thought to be a witch too. She learned me a lot of things. You know the ancient ones in the old country thought a witch or yarb woman was just a wise-woman. Depends on how you think of a witch."

Savannah stepped out into the dooryard and dried her hands on her apron. "Why, Aunt Becky," she said. "You're a sight for sore eyes. Miz Sarah been out of your fine yarbs for nigh onto a week now, and she ain't fit for nothing when I can't make her a bit of yarb tea."

Valor was startled. Savannah had never called anyone "Aunt" in her presence. She always called white females "Miss," or "Miz" if they were married. This woman must be *somebody* for Savannah to

33

use this mountain term of highest respect in speaking to her.

Valor handed the bag to Savannah. "Aunt Becky Linkerfelt," she whispered, remembering what Papa had called her.

"Will you come in and spell yourself by our fire? The kitchen's warm today. Ain't enough wood to keep all the fires going, what with all the men away to the war and all," said Savannah.

"This war." The old woman fairly snorted again. "If men gave birth to new life, they wouldn't be so eager to destroy that life. In war, everybody suffer, and nobody ever wins."

"This goes on much longer, they won't be nobody left to win," said Savannah sadly. "We might nigh to the end of our crops from last year. Spring don't come soon, we going to be mighty hungry."

The old lady nodded in agreement.

"A lot of folks in these parts been hungry this long winter. Some of them done come to me to help them forage. But most don't know the old ways, and they don't seem to want to learn. I helps them as asks." The old lady shook her head sadly.

Savannah nodded again. "You heard any news of the war? Word is mighty hard to come by up here on this mountain."

"Not much word about," replied the lady, "except Caroline Wiseman's man, Zeb, was killed last month. And some of the boys from down at Elsie are being held in a prison camp summers in Georgy."

Valor found herself listening to the quiet canter of the lady's voice without really hearing the words.

"Poor Miz Caroline," said Savannah. "Is her boy, Galen, old enough to run the farm yet?"

"I hear he's talking about jining up and leaving too. I don't know what Miz Caroline will do." The old woman continued, "Any word of Captain John or Sary's brother—Joe or the boys?"

"Miz Sarah gets a letter once in a while. As far as we know, they all be in one piece. Jeff is with Master Joe up in Pennsylvany. Master John and Tom both in Virginny."

"It's getting on toward suppertime. I best be starting home," said the old woman, pushing herself up to stand on the wall. She stepped into the saddle, and swung the stallion around. She looked down at Valor across the stone wall.

"Little Sister, freedom be yours only when you give it to yourself. Nobody else can make you free. That's something you have to give to yourself. And giving it takes great courage." She paused. "Being free inside, especially for a woman, being free will make you different. That's a high price to pay, but

35

giving yourself freedom makes you a sister to the wind.''

She spurred the stallion and galloped down the ridge road. Valor stood as still as a fence post staring after her, the old woman's words echoing inside her head.

"Wait, Auntie," called Savannah. "We owes you for these yarbs." She stopped and turned back toward the kitchen. "Just like her. Never will take a thing for her yarbs. If she be a witch-woman, she be the biggest-hearted one hereabouts."

Valor continued to stare at the spot where the woman had disappeared into the thicket that surrounded the cliffs of the south ridge. She could not hear Savannah's voice over the words still ringing inside her head.

"Miss Vallie," Savannah commanded, "stop wool-gathering. They's wood to be carried. You'd think that old witch-woman done flummoxed you the way she did that fair David-man long time ago. Get your mind back to that woodpile. I've got supper to fix." Savannah turned back to her work, muttering, "Wisht I knowed how she weave that cloth so soft like a cloud and what berries she use to get her yarn that color. Even if it be witch-spell, it sure be a bonny hue."

Valor made her way back to the woodpile, but in her mind she was riding a gray stallion, her cape flying behind her, galloping from mountaintop to mountaintop, a sister to the wind.

CHAPTER 3

The spring nights were still cold, but the days were warming. The forsythia was in bloom, and the fragrance of narcissus and daffodil announced that planting time was soon to come. Cool nights invited mountain children out to hunt boomers and squirrels, meat to enrich the spare spring diet when the root cellars and smokehouses were almost empty.

"Vallie, throw that rope over here," whispered Jed, standing on top of the dooryard wall that spring. "Over the limb, not over Aunt Sarah's trellis. It'll fall."

"Cousin Jed, I *am* trying. Give me time," said Valor. She hoped that Savannah was still back in the summer kitchen behind the house so she would not hear. The warm days would soon be upon them, so all the cooking would be done in a small building in back of the house in order to keep the house cool.

"Shep, be quiet." A golden collie barked and jumped up on the porch, trying to reach Valor's feet where they dangled through the rails of the balcony.

"What you two be doing out here in the dead of night?" came a deep, rich voice from the porch stairs.

"I just . . ." stammered Valor, pulling her feet up through the rails. "Savannah, please don't tell Mama."

"Slipping out to hunt with that cousin of yours, I'll vow." Savannah walked out on the porch and stood towering, her broad shoulders filling the doorway, her skin blue-black in the light of the lantern Jed had set on the steps. Savannah's brown eyes narrowed under the faded gray kerchief she wore tied around her head, as Jed dropped out of sight.

"Jed Burl, come back over that wall. I done cotched you again. Into the house, the both of you, before I wake Miz Sarah and tell her what you'uns is up to."

"Oh, Sav," whined Jed, climbing back over the wide stone wall. "You know Aunt Sarah'd have us tanned for sure."

"Lordy, I reckon. It ain't fittin' for a female young'un of nigh onto eleven years to go traipsing off into the woods in broad daylight, much less in

39

the pitch-black of night!'' Savannah glowered down at Jed, who was short for his ten years. But Valor stayed out of sight in the shadows of the balcony.

"Now, get yourselves back to your rooms. When I check, I wants to find both of you asleep," said Savannah.

"Tomorrow night we go," whispered Valor.

"No, you won't, Young Missy," said Savannah.

Savannah often said she could hear the corn growing in the summertime, and Valor believed her. No secret was safe around Savannah.

"Ever since you come here, Young Missy been in trouble," Savannah said. "Your pa off fighting for the North. Ain't no reason for you to be sent to us good Confederate folks."

Valor sat on the balcony floor just out of Savannah's sight. She hoped that Jed didn't hear Savannah's last words. Her cousin had come to live with her family when his mother died from typhoid fever the winter past. The farm on top of Buck Hill had been very lonely before he came. Since Papa and her older brothers had been away, she liked having Jed around, even if he was a Yankee.

Valor's papa was a Reb, and whatever her papa was, Valor was. Now that Valor was older, she knew all about her brothers and her uncle, too. Her two brothers were fighting on opposite sides. Jeff,

40

the older brother, had joined Jed's father, her uncle Joe, in the 13th Tennessee Cavalry, United States of America. Tom, the younger brother, had joined Papa in the 49th North Carolina regiment, Confederate States of America.

Sometimes Valor and Jed argued about who was in charge of the farm while her father was away. Jed said he was the person in charge because it was the mountain way for men to be in charge. He argued that he was the only man around except Ben and that Ben couldn't be in charge because he was a slave.

Valor said that Ben had been freed and that she was in charge because she was the oldest child of the owner on the farm. Jed said she didn't count because she was a girl.

Valor got very angry when Jed said that. She knew that it was the mountain way that women could inherit and own land. Someday she might be the owner of her father's farm, so she could not understand why she could not be in charge. If Jed wanted to bring his flatland ways with him, believing that women did not count, Valor would just have to teach him the ways of the mountains and change his mind.

Being the only girl in a houseful of older brothers had been difficult enough when she was little, but having a *younger* boy around to remind her constantly that men were stronger and wiser made Valor angry. Her brothers might be bigger and stronger, but she knew she was as smart as they were. And a lot stronger and smarter than a flatland cousin who thought that boys were more important than girls.

"But I'm older," she told Jed. "And taller."

"It doesn't matter that you are older. You are still a girl. I'm the man. I'm in charge until Uncle John comes home," he retorted.

But it did matter. As Valor reminded him every chance she got.

It mattered to Valor that Jed did not value her because she was a girl, just as it mattered that Jed did not value her papa's medal just because it was not awarded from the whole U.S. Army. She knew she had value whether she was a boy or a girl, and she knew her papa's medal was valuable or he would not have given it to her to remind her to have courage.

One day just after Jed came to live on the hill farm, he and Valor had their only fight. It was about Papa's medal. Valor had pinned the medal to her coat, and Jed had laughed at her.

"Wearing that old medal doesn't mean Uncle John had courage. It's not even a real Army medal.

My papa says the U.S. Army doesn't have medals for valor or anything else," Jed had said.

"It does too mean something," Valor had responded. "My papa's captain gave it to him out in Texas. He was very brave."

"My papa says that medals mean kings and queens in other countries. He says they won't ever be a part of this country," Jed had argued, until Valor was angry at him.

"My papa says his captain came from another country. They have medals there. He told Papa that brave men deserve a mark of honor, so he had the smithy at the fort make medals for men like my papa. *Very brave men!*" Valor had shouted at her cousin.

"That old medal don't mean anything!" Jed shouted back, as Valor leaped on him and knocked him to the ground.

Savannah had pulled them apart and threatened to tan both their hides if she caught them fighting again. Valor had run to cover the medal with her handkerchief in the drawer of the bureau in her room.

Jed's words still smarted a year later, so Valor never allowed him to see her papa's medal again. She wore it pinned to her shift under her shirt. She knew it was real or Papa would not have given it to her.

And she never reminded Jed that *his* papa did not have such a wonderful medal to give him.

But when Valor and Jed argued, the subject was not the war or whether the North or South was right. Every day that she remembered the danger the war could bring to her family, she decided all over again that whatever the cause, war was a useless waste of time. Besides, Valor could not imagine anything that was important enough to take the people she loved away for such a long time. Jed did not agree, so he and Valor only argued about *really* important things, such as the best way to skin a rabbit or whether to roast or fry the trout they caught in the creek.

Valor was remembering the smell of trout cooked over the fire on the creek bank as she tiptoed over to the edge of the balcony. Maybe they should wait to go fishing tomorrow instead.

On the porch below, Savannah was giving Jed "what-for." Savannah's what-fors were to be avoided. Normally, the woman was an island of calm and peace, but her words could sting the heart like the sleet that stung their cheeks when the gray of winter mantled the hilltop farm.

"Aw, Savannah," wailed Jed, climbing back over the high stone wall that loomed on the south side of the big farmhouse. "We were only going to the barn. Charlotte's getting ready to foal. I promised Valor we could help.''

"Lordy, Lordy, child, I reckon. Hain't fittin' fer a young lady to witness the birthing of no beast. Valor is a proper lady, and she ain't going to be part of no mare's birthing.''

Valor forgot she was eavesdropping. "Savannah, Papa promised me Charlotte's foal for my birthday next,'' she called. Then she leaned over the balcony rail to hang from her knees until her face was upside down directly in front of Savannah's.

"Get down here this minute, Valor Matilda McAimee, afore you waken your ma. She sees you a-hanging upside down like that, she'll have a set-back even pennyrile tea won't cure,'' said Savannah. "Get down here this instant.''

Valor swung herself down to the porch to face Savannah. Savannah was shocked at what she saw. "Lordy me! Child,'' she said, "what air you doing, wearing yore pappy's britches? Who let you do that? Lordy, Lordy. What is this house a-coming to?''

"I let me, Savannah. I gave myself the freedom to wear britches, and we're only going down to the barn. I want to be there when Charlotte's foal is born. When I have my own horse, then I can really be a sister to the wind,'' said Valor, remembering the old wise-woman's words.

45

But she didn't tell Savannah that when she put on her pa's britches she didn't feel so small and frightened anymore. If only she were not told to be quiet and ladylike all the time, she might prove she was as smart and strong as her brothers, so she wouldn't have to live with the terror. She would find the red-bearded man who had haunted her dreams for the past two years. Then she would hurt him as he had hurt her mama. Valor thought she would like to take him away from his family, just as he had taken her sweet, happy mother by hurting her and causing her to sit all day staring out the window.

Sometimes Valor closed her eyes and remembered how happy her family had been before the war. Papa, Ben, and her brothers had worked hard to provide food. Savannah and Sarah had worked hard, cooking, preserving, sewing, knitting, and cleaning. But almost every night after supper, Papa brought out his banjo, Ben rosined up the bow to his fiddle, Jeff played his harmonica, and Tom twanged his jaw harp as music filled the house in the meadow. Sometimes, Papa and Ben played while Valor, her mother, and her brothers danced the reels and contradances brought by their grandparents from the old country. Valor's papa believed that happy music was for every day, not to be saved for Saturday nights.

Sarah and Savannah sang as they gathered on the porch in the summertime and around the fireplace in the big front room in the winter. Sometimes she remembered Papa putting down his banjo and lifting Valor high in his strong arms to dance with her as he sang her favorite song,

"The gypsy rover came over the hill,
And down through the green wood so shady.
He whistled and sang 'til the green wood rang,
And he won the heart of a lady.
Ah dee do. Ah dee do da day.
Ah dee do, ah dee daisy.
He whistled and sang 'til the green wood rang,
And he won the heart of a lady."

Valor, lost in remembering the good times before the war, reached up and touched Papa's medal hidden beneath her shirt. Wearing it reminded her to have courage, just as Papa had said it would.

Valor's mind snapped back into the present as she heard Savannah say, "Miss Valor, 'til your mammy's ill health is past, and 'til your pappy's done returned from the war, you are going to do what I say. And if I say you be a *lady,* you gonna be a lady!" Savannah said, stamping her foot and placing one fist on each hip. "Even if you be as stubborn as a mule."

When Savannah put one hand on each hip, Valor knew she would get what-for and that no argument could sway the woman in whose care her father had entrusted their lives when he went away to fight for the Confederate States of America.

"Savannah, please," pleaded Valor. "Please let me go."

"I have spoke," said Savannah. "Jedediah Burl, off to bed with you, too. Old Ben'll see to Charlotte and the horses. To bed, Miss Valor. And that dog has no place in a lady's room."

Savannah shook a long finger at Jed and grabbed a handful of Shep's coat. She opened the storage room door and pushed the big dog inside.

"The woods be full of Yankee renegades. I heard tell they's marauders scouting the countryside, as well as the home Yankees. Like that pappy of yours, being a traitor."

"My pa's not a traitor," said Jed. "He says the South can't win the war, and he don't believe in it nohow."

"Changing sides to fight again' his own wife's family and blood kin. Lordy, Lordy. What's this world a-coming to in this war?"

Savannah rocked back and forth in the doorway, shaking her head.

"And don't you let on to your ma what's happened, Miss Valor. She's doin' poorly enough, what with no letter from your pa in a fortnight or so," Savannah continued, off in her own thoughts. "Our men getting whipped has almost done your ma in. Your papa's last letter was not a help. I'm afraid she ain't going to mend until this old war is over and all her men be safe at home."

Jed stood on one foot, then the other.

"Savannah, won't you let me go see the birthin'? I saw the sow have a litter plenty of times," argued Jed.

"I want to go too," said Valor.

"Miss Valor, the only place you be going is up to bed, as fast as you can climb them stairs," said Savannah in a voice that was not to be argued with. But her words were cut short by hoofbeats coming around the curve of the hill. In the bright moonlight, eight riders wearing uniforms were galloping up the road.

"Are they Rebs or Yankees?" asked Valor, fear almost choking her.

The riders were still too far away to recognize, but Valor was sure she saw a bright red beard. Every time the soldiers came, Valor felt the terror rising in her throat. Then her pulse began to race as she felt panic, then anger, take over her body.

Each time the soldiers came, Valor would waken

the following night screaming with nightmares, so that Savannah would come running up the stairs to light Valor's candle. Then Savannah would sit and hold her hand until again she slept.

"Can't see yet," said Jed. "It looks like they're Yankees."

Savannah's voice was quiet and cold. "Get inside," she commanded. Valor felt the terror again even though that night in the closet had happened more than a year ago.

Jed and Valor pushed through the doorway to hide behind the door. Then, silently, they peeped out. Valor grasped Papa's medal where she wore it pinned to her shift inside Papa's shirt. She could see the first man, wearing a broad blue hat, as he reined in. He was followed by seven others. The soldiers stopped at the gate in the stone wall. Valor looked from one face to the other, her fist clenched. She felt so helpless.

"Someday I'll find him," she whispered. "I will remember."

"Evenin', ma'am," the man called out, tipping his hat. "We're looking for . . ."

"That ain't no ma'am. That's nothing but a slave," said the man behind him. "Just a sla—"

Savannah interrupted him. "I be a free woman. Given my freedom on papers by my master," she said in a voice like stone. "And he give me the duty of looking after his kin. And I mean to 'bide by that."

"Who is your master?" asked the soldier in the broad hat.

"Colonel Joh—" Valor started to say.

"Colonel Joe Burl, U.S. Army," Jed interrupted, stepping from behind Savannah. "Forty-ninth Regiment. He's my pa."

Valor's anger at Jed rose in her throat, but she did not speak.

"Home Yankees," laughed the soldier. "I was told this was a Reb farm."

"You'd have to look hard to find a Reb here," said Jed. "We told you, Pa even freed Savannah on papers."

"You'd best be speaking the truth, son," said the soldier. "Then we'll be passing on through. Only needing some corn for the horses. We'll move on to some Reb place and take some there."

"Good evenin', sir," said Savannah with great dignity.

"Good evenin', ma'am," said the soldier, sarcastically. He lifted his hat, pulled on the reins, and wheeled his horse around. He led his men around the curve and off the mountain.

Savannah, Jed and Valor stood in silence, but

Valor's heart drowned out the sound of the hoof-beats. Finally, her fear turned to anger at the war, at the men who hurt her family, the men who brought on her mother's silence.

Then she remembered.

"Red Beard," she whispered, shaking her fist toward the north slope road where she had first seen him riding so long ago. "I will remember. I will have my own horse. I will be a sister to the wind. Then, look out. I will find you."

CHAPTER 4

The next morning, the scent of apple blossoms wafted through the open doorway as Savannah lifted the big black coffeepot from its hook in the fireplace to pour steaming liquid into a black iron skillet where ham sizzled in its own juices. Cathead biscuits were browning in the round oven banked with hot coals on the floor of the fireplace. Their fragrance blended with the pungent almost-coffee odor of dried chicory root.

Valor came running into the summer kitchen, which was attached to the main house by a covered walkway, slapping her arms to warm them, her breath like smoke rising in the air.

"Savannah. Savannah. The foal still hasn't been born! Charlotte is having trouble of some kind. Old Ben says I can help. . . ."

"Charlotte don't need no help from you a-birthing a foal. Now, set down here. Your breakfast is might nigh done," said Savannah.

"Where's Jed?" asked Valor.

"He went off to check the stock. Them Yankee filth may have been marauders, tried to make off with your pappy's stock," said Savannah. "Eat hearty, Miss Valor. Ben said he can use an extra hand shucking the last of that corn. It has to go to mill to be ground. Then you gonna tie up the rest of that fodder for the cows."

"A lady has to keep her hands pretty, Mama says," said Valor, tossing her brown curls and holding her hands up to examine them. She hated for Mama and Savannah to remind her to be a lady, but sometimes their reminders made good excuses. Being a lady did not appeal to her, but cutting fodder had even less appeal. She tried again. "Fodder cuts my hands all to pieces."

"A lady don't hang from her heels upside down neither," said Savannah with a snort, placing a pan of hot biscuits on the table. "And a lady don't wear her pappy's pants. And a lady don't slip out after night to go a-hunting. But a lady can cut fodder when the men's away, and they's work needing doing."

Valor poured molasses out of the pitcher into her plate, plopped a pat of butter into the brown pool, and stirred the brown and yellow until they were mixed. She grabbed a biscuit and, breaking it, she crumbled it into the mixture. She began to spoon great chunks into her mouth, molasses dripping down her chin.

"Miss Valor, when you gonna learn to eat dainty like a lady, and not like a Yankee pig?" said Savannah, setting a steaming cup by Valor's plate.

"That's how you and Ben eat sorghum. It's good that way," said Valor, mumbling through her food.

"And I ain't no lady. I be a free woman. And my mammy ain't worried about me growing up a wild mountain thing either," said Savannah. "You are, and you gonna be, or your mammy gonna skin you and me both alive when she get better, fer not a-training you to be a lady."

"I don't want to be a lady. I wish I could leave here. I want to be like Jed and go find that man who hurt my mama and made her sick. I want to be a soldier so I can fight that awful man who came here to hurt us!" She slammed her cup on the table. "I want to see the world over mountaintops and help to stop this war and bring my papa home."

"Miss Valor, you just shut your mouth. Miz Sarah might hear you. She done had another bad night," said Savannah. A reminder of her mother's illness brought Valor back to earth. She grew quiet.

"How is Mama today?" asked Valor, feeling the familiar knot in her stomach at the mention of her mother's illness. "I went by this morning, but she was still sleeping."

"Ain't took her tray up yet. But she was finally a-sleeping peaceful as a baby when I looked in on her afore I started breakfast. She didn't sleep 'til might nigh daylight," said Savannah.

"When's Mama going to be well again? I miss the way she used to be. I want Mama back the way she was!" said Valor.

Savannah made a clicking sound with her tongue. "Lordy, ain't no tellin'," said Savannah, shaking her head sadly. "Seems like since that last baby died after her fall, the life just went out of her. She ain't never seen a well minute since."

Valor closed her eyes. She could still see the red-bearded man as he pushed her mother causing her to fall down the stairs. "I remember," said Valor, swallowing her feelings. She quickly changed the subject, hoping Savannah would not guess how small and frightened she felt.

"Will Mama have any more babies? Now that Tom and Jeff are gone off to war, only I'm left. If we had a new baby around here, maybe we would not feel so sad when we remember the baby Mama lost that night. Another baby might help Mama get well again."

"Lordy, Lordy, Miss Valor," said Savannah, lifting her hands to the sky and praying softly. "Oh, Lord, help me find a way to tell Miss Valor without telling her things a lady ought not to know."

Finally she put her hands on the back of the chair opposite Valor.

"Honey, you old enough to know your pa ain't been home in nigh onto two years. Don't know how's a lady can't rightly get a baby with no man around."

"Oh, I know all about that," said Valor. "I helped old Ben breed Charlotte when she . . ."

"Lordy, Lordy, child," said Savannah wringing her hands. "You ain't got no call to be doing them things. Ladies ain't supposed to. I wish your ma would hurry and get well, so she's could teach you how to be a lady. I ain't doing sich a good job of it, I reckon."

"I told you I don't want to be a lady," said Valor. "I want to be a sister to the wind. I want to be like Aunt Becky, the wise-woman."

Shaking her head, Savannah busily laid the breakfast tray. Then she cut a pat of butter, split a biscuit, buttered it and placed a slice of red salt-cured ham inside the biscuit.

Jed came running into the kitchen. Shep was at his side. "Savannah, two riders are coming up the road."

"Be they soldiers again?" asked Savannah, walking toward the door.

"They ain't wearing uniforms," said Jed. "Ben told me to get back to the barn. He needs me there." The boy jumped off the porch and leaped over the gate, turning around to open it for Shep to follow.

Savannah walked out to the porch rail and shaded her eyes from the morning sun with her hand. "It appears to be the Blaylocks, the one they call Keith. Ain't no man in this county the size of him," said Savannah. "Lordy, Lordy. Let me water the gravy a mite," she said. "They's biscuit enough."

The two riders stopped by the kitchen gate and dismounted. One of them, a huge man with shoulders like those of an ox, tied the reins to the wooden fence. His brown beard and bushy hair made a fine frame for his ruddy face and dancing brown eyes.

He was followed by a lady, taller than most, wearing a short riding skirt. Her brown curls barely touching her shoulders glistened in the sun.

"My, he's a handsome man," said Valor, giggling.

"Shhh, he'll hear you," whispered Savannah.

The man led the way to the gate in the stone fence, opened it and led the lady through. She smiled up at her giant of a husband. Shep wandered back through the gate, pushing his way between the pair.

"Howdy, folks," said Savannah. "Come in and spell yourselves. Mistress right poorly, so she ain't riz yet, but coffee's on, such as it is, and bread's a-baking. You're right welcome."

"We just stopped to spell the horses," said Mr. Blaylock. "We're on our way to Caroline Wiseman's. Word just came to us that her man was killed at Fort Donelson. It took more than a month for word to reach her. Word sure travels slow. And then on to the English farm down river."

"And to ask about Sarah," added Mrs. Blaylock. Valor noticed how pretty the lady was.

"A cup of coffee would taste mighty fine," said Mr. Blaylock. "Mighty fine."

"It ain't for-sure coffee," said Savannah. "It's burnt chicory root all ground up. But it'll have to do in these times."

"It's better than what we have up on Grandfather

Mountain." Mrs. Blaylock laughed. "I tried roasting bayberries and using them for coffee."

"It ain't coffee, but it'll have to do. At least it's better than what we had in the Army of the Confederacy," said Mr. Blaylock. "The hardships them men is suffering . . . but a cup would be mighty fine, if'n it ain't too much to trouble you, Savannah."

Savannah stood back so they could come into the kitchen. Each of the Blaylocks took off a dusty hat and hung it on the peg by the door.

"If'n you'll stay a spell, I'll open up the sitting room, and spread the eatin'-table for you," said Savannah. "With Master gone, and Miz Sarah sick and all, these young'uns, Ben, and me, we just eat here in the summer kitchen nowadays."

"Kitchen's fine," said Mrs. Blaylock. "We don't want to put you out."

"Put us out," snorted Savannah. "Miss Valor and me, we're glad to have company. It do get lonesome up here on this mountain. News is slow in reaching us too. We're pretty fur off the main roads."

"Be glad," said Mr. Blaylock. "With marauders about, a feller ain't safe in his own bed, if he's lucky enough to have one."

Valor helped Savannah set the plates on the table and spoon the food into serving bowls.

"You don't have a bed?" said Valor. "Where do you sleep?"

"We have our cabin fixed up nice now. We have straw ticks instead of the floor. Course we have to be careful when we light the fire, so the smoke won't give us away," said Mrs. Blaylock.

"We're still hiding," said Mr. Blaylock, as they sat down, one on each side of the table. "We're thought to be deserters."

"I heard you was mustered out, all legal-like," said Savannah, passing a bowl of fried apples to Mr. Blaylock first, as was the mountain custom. "These Jonathans make fine sase," she said. "Won't you have some?"

"We was, and I will," said Mr. Blaylock, helping himself to the fried apples dripping with butter.

"But they're some folks—on both sides—that feel that what we done was wrong. So we keep hid, except among friends."

"You must be hard to hide," said Valor, giggling. Savannah glowered at her. "I mean you must be the biggest man in the county."

"Mayhap, missy." Mr. Blaylock smiled. He winked at Valor as each Blaylock piled a plate high and began to eat as if food had not been plentiful for them.

"How's the crops up Montezuma way?" asked

61

Savannah. "Ours was a mite poorly again last year, what with no men on the place to work them. Our taters just didn't make at all. This is the third year of bad crops. Another'n like this, and we may all us'uns starve."

"If marauders don't burn us out, we'll make it through the rest of winter, but just barely," said Mrs. Blaylock. "I'm glad to see spring come this year."

"But you're better off than some," said Mr. Blaylock. "Marauders stole all the stock from some farms over to Foscoe. Only one man had a team of oxen to plow. He plowed for everybody on the New River last year, or the whole valley would have starved."

"Soldiers butchered all the hogs and chickens in the valley. Took the cows along to resupply the troops. Left those poor people with nothing to eat. Some of the babies died of starvation, and lots of folks went hungry through last winter," said Mrs. Blaylock.

"Lordy, Lordy," said Savannah, shaking her head. "What make men want to have wars any-how?"

"Some say we're fighting to have some say-so in whether we have slaves or not. Others say we fight-ing to hold the Union together when it has already done fell apart," said Mr. Blaylock, shaking his head sadly.

"It's my guess most folks don't know why they're fighting. Everybody else, their friends and family, joined up and most folks joined them. But everybody's suffering," said Mrs. Blaylock. "War makes no sense at all, it seems to me."

"We be luckier than most, being off the main road up here on the hill," said Savannah. "We've seen soldiers from both sides, but so far we have all our livestock except old Daisy, the cow that died." She stopped. "Which side the marauders on?"

"Either and neither," said Keith Blaylock. "They're renegades from both sides. Some hide from one army or the other—foraging and pillaging to stay alive. Sometimes I think they burn and loot out of cussed meanness."

"But they hit their friends along with the foes," said Melinda Blaylock. "They don't seem to choose the people they aim their wrath at. They just aim it at everybody the same."

Valor's blue eyes widened with fear. She felt her own wrath after the pain the red-bearded man had caused her family.

"I hear the Yankees burned the Chambers house at Altamont," said Savannah. "That was the finest house I ever seed."

63

"Word is that Colonel Chambers had burned Colonel Kirk's mother's home up in Virginia, so Kirk settled that point by burning Chambers' home-place at Altamont," said Mr. Blaylock. "Got any more them biscuits, Savannah? They're mighty fine."

Valor felt her anger pass. She sat quietly for a moment and finally she blurted out the question she had wanted to ask since the visitors arrived. "Mrs. Blaylock, is it true you passed as a man and joined the army?"

Savannah glowered at Valor. "That's no question to ask a lady, Miss Valor," said Savannah.

But Mrs. Blaylock smiled at Valor and put her hand on her husband's big shoulder.

"It's a fact," she said. "Me and my man ain't been separated—not even for a night since we got married. And no war was gonna take him from me."

"Lordy, Lordy," mumbled Savannah from the fireplace. "What tales to be telling this headstrong child."

"Keith, why don't you tell her about my army days while I go check on Sarah?" said Mrs. Blaylock. "Do you think I could take her tray, Savannah?"

"That would please her mightily, Miz Blaylock,"

said Savannah. "You'll be a sight for sore eyes. Let me fix her tray."

Savannah bustled about, placing three ham biscuits and a bowl of fried apples beside a small pot and a cup on the tray.

"Here it is," she said. "First door on the right, down the hall."

Valor watched Mrs. Blaylock walk down the hall. *She's a woman, and she went to war,* she thought, tapping one foot against the floor in excitement. *She wore britches and her husband is proud of her. I'll bet she rides astride too. I'll bet Papa would be right proud of me if I did that, too.* She stopped her foot from tapping, as a new thought occurred to her.

I'll bet she is a sister to the wind! Like the old wisewoman. And like me, too. A sister to the wind!

CHAPTER 5

"Any news of how the war be going?" asked Savannah.

"Word came last week down to Morganton that Stonewall Jackson be marching his men up the Shenandoah on his way to take Washington. But there ain't no way the South can win this war. All this suffering is for naught," Mr. Blaylock answered.

"Lordy, Lordy," said Savannah. "Let it be over soon."

"Now, young lady, you want to hear about 'Sam' Blaylock? Is that it?" asked Mr. Blaylock, leaning back in his chair, his chest swelling with pride. Like Valor, he knew that a mountain woman would be far too modest to boast. If boasting was to be done, her husband would have to do it.

Valor sat at the table. Mr. Blaylock took a swig

of the chicory brew, set his cup down, and began his story.

"Well, we had just been married when the war broke out. I didn't see no point in war, but the conscript law was passed. I couldn't get out of it." The big man laughed. "So Mel decided she would join too. And I'm right proud she did."

"How did she do that?" asked Valor.

"First she cut off her hair so she looked like just a snip of a boy. Hair ain't full growed out yet," he said. "Then she cut down some old clothes of mine. That took some cutting"—he laughed again—"and made them fit her."

He paused for a moment. "Then she went with me to join Zeb Vance's 26th North Carolina Volunteers. They was so short of men, they didn't ask too many questions. Anybody old enough to march could join up. She signed up as 'Sam Blaylock,' my younger brother. Plenty a young boys ain't shaved yet in the 26th. She passed all right. They assigned us to a tent together, so nobody was the wiser."

"Did she shoot and fight?" asked Valor.

"She was already a fair shot. She drilled and practiced just like a man. Mel always was good with a gun. But she never had to kill in battle, thank the Lord. We finally figured out we was fighting for the losing side and wanted out."

"What did you do?" asked Valor, sitting on the edge of her chair, resting her arms on the table.

"Well, it is hard to believe, but I found me a patch of pizen oak, and I fair wallered in it. Then I broke out all over. Course I knew it would dry up in a couple of weeks, but them Reb doctors didn't expect anybody to do such a fool thing as that. It did not dawn on them, so they couldn't figure out what was wrong with me. They sent me home, hoping nobody else'd catch it."

He leaned back, clasped his hands behind his head, and laughed out loud. "Them Reb doctors," he said. "You would think they would know pizen oak, but they did not."

"What did Sam, uh, Mrs. Blaylock do next?" asked Valor.

"She proved to Zeb Vance she was Melinda," said Mr. Blaylock. "She . . ."

Savannah interrupted him. "And didn't that pizen oak itch?"

"Yep, but it passed pretty soon." He chuckled. "Still can't believe I fooled them Reb doctors."

"And you got out of the Army like that?" asked Valor. "I wish Pa would do something so he could come home. Do you think they have poison oak in Virginia where Pa is, Mr. Blaylock?"

"Hush your mouth, Miss Valor. Your pa's fighting fer his land. He ain't no Tory, no dirty home Yankee, like some as I could name," said Savannah.

"Uncle Joe is not a Tory. He's fighting on the Union side. That saved our lives yesterday," said Valor, surprised that she felt a need to defend Jed's actions or her uncle.

"Lordy, Lordy. The tongue in that young'un! What is the world coming to, talking again' your pa?" Savannah shook her kerchiefed head.

"Well, Savannah, it's surprising to hear you talk that way. I thought you'd be a Unionist."

Savannah drew herself up to her full height. She towered over the huge man as he sat at the table. Her kerchief almost touched the rafters. She placed a hand on each hip. Valor smiled. She knew that no matter how big he was, Mr. Blaylock was going to get Savannah's what-for.

"Mr. Blaylock, I done be a free woman. Miz Sarah's pappy give me papers fer saving Miz Sarah's life when she was just a bit of a thing. And Ben be a free man too. This be our home. We is free. This be our family, the only family we know."

"I know. I know, Savannah," said Mr. Blaylock. "Everybody hereabouts knows you free."

"I be a free woman," said Savannah proudly. "Not a slave."

"All right, a free woman," said Mr. Blaylock.

"But you know the South's gonna lose this war. Ain't no way they can win. John's fighting fer the wrong side. Now Sarah's brother, Joe, he got smart, and changed sides. Must be tough on Sarah."

"Ma says she's loyal to neither side," said Valor. "She just wants the war to be over so everybody can come home."

"Lots of mountain families tore apart in this war. Wounds won't heal for years," said Mr. Blaylock. They sat for a moment in silence.

"That reminds me. Where is Joe's boy since Joe's wife died?" Mr. Blaylock continued.

Savannah lifted a pot from its hook in the fireplace and placed it on the cabinet. Then she poured steaming water into the pot and began to scrub.

"Young Jed's staying with us 'til his pa gets home," said Savannah, placing the baking pans into the water and scrubbing away.

Mr. Blaylock laughed. "Savannah, do you have a war around here between these two with their pas fighting on opposite sides?"

"Jed and Miss Valor been playing together ever since they born. Ain't no war gonna change that!" Savannah sniffed.

"Is Jed still in the barn with Ben?" asked Valor.

"He's been there since sunup. Go tell Ben to

bring him up to the house. That boy has to eat," said Savannah.

Valor jumped off the high summer-kitchen porch and cleared the gate with one leap.

"That young'un won't ever learn to be a lady," sighed Savannah.

"May be more to being a lady than just being prim and proper," said Keith Blaylock.

Savannah raised one eyebrow and turned back to her pots.

As Valor skipped through the meadow, her heart danced along with her feet. There were two other women she knew who wore britches, and one of them had gone off to the war. She jumped high into the air and spun around, raising her arms and lifting her face to the sun. She felt happier than she had in a long time, suddenly free of the fear and anger that had caused her spirits to sag like the hemlocks by the south wall sodden with heavier winter ice. Spring had come, not only to the meadow, but to her soul as well. Life was indeed a joyous thing, now that she knew there were three women who were sisters to the wind. And Valor knew that she was one of them. A sister to the wind.

CHAPTER 6

Valor and Shep ran down the slope and across the
meadow toward the barn. Picking up her skirts and
petticoats on each side of her body, Valor tossed
them over her forearm so they were not in the way
of her legs when she ran. Then, as it happened
almost every time she went through the gap, fear
rose in her throat. She looked up expecting to see
the red-bearded man riding toward her. But no one
was there. She did not want the glorious morning
ruined, so she pushed her fear away by singing the
song Pa used to sing to her. She began to sing,

"The gypsy rover came over the hill,
And down through the valley so shady.
He whistled and sang 'til the green wood rang,
And he won the heart of a lady."

Every time she saw Valor running, Savannah scolded her.

"A lady never lets a soul see her ankles," said Savannah. But long skirts got in Valor's way.

Valor felt less fear if she pretended she was big and strong like Papa. Somehow wearing his pants made her feel less like a small frightened child. So she wore Papa's pants when no one could see her. "Why can't I wear britches like Jed?" she had asked when she was ten.

"'Cause it ain't fittin' for a lady," said Savannah. "Lordy, Lordy. A gal-child a-wantin' to wear britches. What is this world coming to?"

But Valor had never figured out why britches or a skirt made a difference. If britches made her feel strong and brave, she did not understand why she could not wear them. The old wise-woman wore them. She had asked Mama, but Mama had just smiled and said, "Because ladies don't wear them, darling. That's why. They *simply* don't." And Sarah had gone back to her embroidery. So Valor never had an answer.

Since her mother had been confined to her bedroom, Valor sometimes slipped into the tack room, where her father kept his riding pants, and put them on to go riding with Jed, or to slip out hunting at night. Until last night, she had kept her secret from Savannah.

Valor ran down the rocky slope to the gray log barn still singing, "And he won the heart of a lady."

The double doors stood open. Valor walked through the fresh straw Ben had spread on the floor and opened the door to Charlotte's stall. Shep followed her to lie in the corner. The mare's sides heaved as she made an effort to breathe. Ben knelt beside the chestnut horse. Jed stroked the mare's heaving withers.

Valor knelt to examine Charlotte's front hooves. She looked for the tiny "M" Ben so carefully fashioned into the frog of each horseshoe he made in his smithy's shed. When they were children, Valor and Jed liked to pretend they were trackers following the imprint of the "M" whenever horses from the McAimee farm stepped in mud or soft clay.

"Missy, get back!" scolded Ben. Valor was startled. Ben rarely spoke above a whisper. "That mare, she's likely to kick when the birthing come. She could hurt you some bad!"

Valor moved to a spot near Charlotte's head. Charlotte heaved forward. Valor jumped back.

"What's wrong with Charlotte?" asked Valor. "Is she sick?"

"Old Charlotte ain't as young as she has been,"

74

said Ben. "Birthing this here foal has been quite a job for her."

"What can I do?" asked Valor.

"Ain't nothing can be done just now," said Ben. "She gonna drop that foal soon. We'uns just stand by."

Charlotte's sides puffed out like the bellows Ben used when in his smithy shed. The horse kicked her legs while her breath came in gasps.

Finally Valor could see the small head as it appeared in the hay at Charlotte's broad rump. The head was surrounded by a soft, filmy covering. Charlotte almost seemed to leap forward, and the foal lay in its bag on the floor.

"Jed, help me break it out!" said Ben sharply. He began to work frantically with the foal. First a hoof and one skinny leg appeared kicking. Then the head came up, shaking from side to side. Charlotte's head reached back over her shoulder, and she licked her baby gently.

"Get back and let her stand," said Ben. The foal put her front legs forward and pushed with her hind legs. Slowly, shakily, she edged forward. Then she lunged to stand on her tiny hooves.

"Now, Miss," said Ben. "Right this minute, you come up here and pet this foal. She gonna be your'n, she have to know you the mistress right away. Come on, now." Valor hesitated, but Ben took her arm.

"She gonna be your'n, you have to tame her now," said Ben.

Gingerly, Valor put one hand out and touched the foal's wet silky mane. She jerked her hand back.

"You have to tame her now, Missy," said Ben.

"Don't be a scaredy cat," said Jed. "She won't bite you."

"I ain't a scaredy cat," said Valor. "She's wet."

"All living things be wet when they born, Missy," said Ben. "That is nature's way of protecting them."

Timidly, Valor stroked the filly. The foal nuzzled her hand. Its lips felt like velvet against her skin. Ben and Jed continued to work on Charlotte, but Ben talked to Valor.

"Now, Missy, put your arm around her neck," he said. "Just let her get the feel of your hands. Let her get the smell of you so she know who you is."

Valor grew braver and put her other hand and arm around the foal's neck.

"Now she know she's your'n," said Ben. "Come, let her nurse. Her mammy's ready."

Ben helped the foal find the mare's teat, and soon the little horse snuggled down by the mare's belly, nursing contentedly.

"What you going to name her, Vallie?" asked Jed.

"I'll name you Sam, I think," said Valor, stroking the foal's side. "For Sam Blaylock, the lady who dared to wear britches and be a soldier."

"Missy, how you be knowing about Sam Blaylock?" asked Ben.

"The Blaylocks are up at the house having breakfast," said Valor.

"Keith Blaylock be up at the house?" said Ben, his eyes growing wide. "He be the best fighter in Burke County, so's they say. Got fists as big as hams. *That* Keith Blaylock's up at the house?"

"Yes, his wife came by to visit Mama," said Valor. "He is *big!*"

"I thought that's who he was. Ben, I need to go up to the house," said Jed. "Charlotte's done with birthing this foal."

"You go, and we may lose this mare," said Ben. "She's one of the best stock Master John's got left since the war. You going to stay right here, young master."

"But I've never seen Keith Blaylock up close. I want to see him," said Jed.

"You ain't seen this horse dead neither. You stay 'til I say you can go."

78

"Aw, Ben," said Jed. "You want to see him too. Please."

"I said we stay here until we are sure this mare's all done, and then we can go," said Ben. "I want you to bring a bucket of water for Charlotte, while we take care of the rest."

Valor sat in the hay near Charlotte's head and stroked the foal's side.

"Young Missy, you go down to the corncrib and get some of that shelled corn for Charlotte. Fix her nose bag and bring it here. I got some things need to be done for Charlotte it ain't fittin' for a young missus to see. You hurry on now," said Ben.

"You want yellow corn or white?" asked Valor.

"White," said Ben. "It's sweeter."

Valor closed the door to the stall softly and latched it with the wooden button and leather thong. Then she made her way to the corncrib at the east end of the barn. She lifted the latch and took the nose bag from the hook on the wall. The scoop stood upright in the barrel of shelled yellow corn. She lifted it, walked to the barrel of white corn, and began to scoop the small white grains into the canvas bag. Then she latched the corncrib door and tied it with the leather thong.

Inside the stall, Charlotte was standing beside

Ben, nuzzling her colt. Ben stroked Charlotte's withers and grinned, his white teeth gleaming against his brown face, shining with sweat.

"Charlotte going to be all right now. She done finished birthing this finest foal I ever did see. And your pappy done writ home saying this foal gonna be Young Missy's horse," he said. "You got yourself one fine little horse, Miss Valor."

"My very own horse, and her name is Sam."

Ben took the nose bag and hung it around Charlotte's head.

"Our job be finished," said Ben. "I done sent Jed up to the house to see our guests. It's about time you and me made our way too. Come along, Missy," said Ben, opening the door to the stall. "Lordy me, I shore am hungry. How about you, Missy?"

"I ate breakfast, Ben, but I guess I am hungry again," said Valor.

She threw one arm around Ben's stooped shoulders. She was as tall as he.

"Now I have a horse of my very own," she said.

"Your very own," said Ben.

Valor grinned at him. Ben slapped his gnarled hands with joy and opened the gate.

Valor picked up her skirts and began to skip. Shep danced happy circles around her.

"I'll beat you to the house," she called over her shoulder as she began to run.

"That one ain't ever gonna learn to be a lady, I reckon," said Ben. "But then, that one's allus been Master John's best. And she get to be more like her pappy every day."

Ben shook his head and smiled at the brown braid bobbing up and down Valor's back as she skipped across the side yard singing,

"Ah dee do. Ah dee do da day.
Ah dee do, ah dee daisy.
He whistled and sang 'til the green wood rang,
And he won the heart of a lady."

CHAPTER 7
(1863)

Through the following year the mountain farm lay peaceful as the summer heat had turned to fall with the first frost painting Big Yellow Mountain and the Black Mountains with reds, oranges, and yellows. Word had come to the hill farm of the South's setback at a place called Gettysburg, but no signs of the war came to the McAimee house to interrupt the harvest. Marauders rarely ventured off the road to the hilltop. Then the December rains came, stripping the branches to gray fingers pointing toward a bright blue winter sky.

Ben had begun to break Valor's horse to the saddle. Sam was the prettiest chestnut filly ever seen on the hill farm. From the day Valor first saddled her, horse and girl were as of one mind. Sam liked nothing more than to run like the wind. Valor liked nothing more than to gallop across the meadows and hills, horse and rider, sisters to the wind.

One bright winter day, Valor dug her heels into Sam's flanks and cleared the rail fence, her skirts and cape ballooning behind Sam's chestnut rump. She was glad her mother had never insisted she wear hoops. Skirts were confining enough.

Valor pulled on the reins and stopped Sam by a stream that trickled through the thick pines and blackberry briars, now still and brown. Shep ran up to nip at Sam's hooves. The breath of the horse made tendrils in the crisp winter air.

Valor clapped her mittened hands to warm them, then placed them both over her mouth and nose so her breath could warm her nose, which felt like an icicle sticking out from her face. Then she pulled off her knitted cap, allowing one long brown braid to fall down her back.

The winter sun gave little warmth, but painted the mountains now snow-covered against a sky shimmering with light. The air was so clear that she could see for miles. The cliffs of Grandfather Mountain were shadows that darkened the outline of blue, so blue it was almost black against a sky the color of a robin's egg. She stood in the stirrups and stretched her arms wide. Then she turned in the other direction to face the Big Yellow Mountain and the two pointed Spear Tops. The wind, now almost still, only ruffled the curls on her forehead, but the cold air stung her cheeks as she reached her hands toward the sun.

Nearby, the Grassy Ridge Bald loomed over the valley below like a dark cat ready to pounce on the house Papa had built in the flat meadow that formed a gap across Buck Hill. The neighbors had taunted John McAimee about the cold winds that would blow away the fine house he had built for his pretty Sarah. But Mama always said that living anywhere down in the valley made her feel closed in tight. So Pa had built the house in the gap of the hills where the view in either direction from the wide porch reached to the far horizon miles away.

Valor gazed at the tall mountains in the distance. She wished she were a bird who had just stopped to rest in flight, a real sister to the wind. She wished that any moment she might soar away to light on some distant peaks.

"Don't worry, Sam. I'll take you with me," she said, patting the horse's shiny chestnut mane. "You and I. We will become the wind."

Sam whinnied and broke into a trot. Valor began whistling a melody, "Ah dee do. Ah dee do da day . . ." Whistling always made her feel better, even if Savannah said it wasn't ladylike.

"Val. Vallie," called Jed, as he ran up the hill, his long sweater blowing behind him. "We can go hunting tonight. Moon'll be full. Late frost has scared the animals in. Might even tree us a 'coon or a possum. Savannah wants Ben to go so's I'll be sure to get a possum for Christmas dinner. Says she's got some sweet taters stored away to go with it."

"Ma don't like possum. I don't either. It's too greasy. She likes quail. I'd rather go along towards evening, try to get a few boomers for squirrel pie." Valor reined Sam in as Jed panted to a stop.

"Val, Josiah English is going possum hunting and he says we can go with him," said Jed. "That way Ben won't go, and you can."

"Did you tell him I'm going?" asked Val.

"Lord, no!" said Jed. "He'd have a fit. Told him my cousin, Valiant, was here for a spell, and he was going with us. You'll have to wear britches and keep quiet so he won't know who you are."

Valor dismounted to look at Jed across the saddle.

"Right now Savannah says you have to come back to the house," he said. "Ben saw some Reb scouts over by the smokehouse a while ago. Says it's dangerous for you to be out here alone. He's already hid the stock in the woods."

"My pa's a Reb soldier. I'm not afraid."

"Val, Savannah says they're bushwhackers. Run away from the army. Nobody's safe with them," said Jed. "Please, Val." He stood on tiptoe to look across the saddle. "Shhh! Val. There they are. Come on."

Valor looked back over her shoulder. Three gray uniforms appeared at the top of the hill. She stuck her toe into the stirrups and leaped into the saddle.

"Here, Jed," she whispered, offering her hand, her heart in her throat. "Up."

Jed took her hand. He stuck his boot into the stirrup under hers, and she pulled him into the saddle behind her.

"Giddup, Sam." Valor dug her heels into the filly's sides. The pair galloped toward the big house, followed by Shep barking in circles behind them. Sam turned the corner by the barnyard. Ben was forking hay into the cow stalls.

"Ben, Reb renegades," said Jed, sliding out of the saddle.

"Stay in the barn. Take that filly into the barn and hide her there," said Ben.

Ben slowly turned back to forking hay. Valor and

Jed took Sam into the stall and closed the door. Quickly, she opened it again to let Shep in.

The riders came into the barnyard. Their uniforms were dirty. Their horses showed their ribs under their skinny hides.

"Howdy, Uncle," said the fat one to Ben.

"Howdy, Master," said Ben, without slowing his movements.

"Boy, whose slave you? We in need of food. Got any hams in that smokehouse?" asked the fat man.

Jed pulled his uncle's broad brimmed hat down over his face and walked out of the shadows.

"His master's my uncle, Captain John McAimee, Confederate States of America, head of Company C, 49th Regiment, North Carolina Infantry," said Jed. "We have no hams. Ain't butchered yet. But we have plenty of sidemeat. Turnips and taters in the cellar, too."

"We're mighty obliged," said the soldier.

"You're welcome to share. Ben, get these men some provisions." Jed spoke as if he commanded an army.

"But, Master Jedediah . . ." said Ben.

"Right away, Ben," said Jed. "We're loyal to the cause and we help any way we can."

Valor climbed into the hayloft to lie down in the

hay where she could look out the door that hung open over the entrance. Her heart was in her throat. Uniforms, either blue or gray, always made Valor remember that awful night when the red-bearded man had changed their lives forever.

"Gentlemen, feel free to set up camp in our sideyard. It's protected from the wind," said Jed, still in his commanding voice.

"We be mighty obliged," said the fat soldier as Ben came out of the smokehouse with a slab of sidemeat.

He handed the meat to the soldier.

"Take the turnips and taters over to their camp," said Jed, turning to Ben.

"Yes, Master Jed," said Ben.

The soldiers rode away. Valor walked forcefully out of the shadows of the doorway, followed by Shep.

"Jed, who gave you the right to give away our food?" sputtered Valor, pretending bravery she did not feel. "Sav says our sidemeat is almost gone. Giving our meat away! We'll all starve. This is not your home. You have no right . . ."

"Miss Valor, renegades is mean. They hungry. Whatever Jed done, he done right," said Ben.

"Vallie, Johnny Rebs ain't going to steal from a Reb farm. But if we don't feed them, they're likely to think we're home Yankees and burn us out," said Jed breathlessly.

"I'll thank you not to pretend this farm's yours," said Valor. "Jed, you are a guest. I'll handle things here. This farm belongs to *my* pa."

Valor picked up her skirts, flung her head haughtily and walked toward the house. She climbed the steps to the summer-kitchen porch, stamping a foot on each step. Suddenly, the leaves of the big boxwood moved, and a gray arm grabbed Valor by the waist.

"Let me go! Put me down!" she screamed. "Jed! Ben! Savannah! Somebody help me." The smell of the man almost suffocated her. She kicked at his boots. He only laughed a hoarse laugh.

"Sir," said Jed, "as our guests, I'll thank you to treat our womenfolk like ladies."

Valor looked over the man's shoulder. Jed and Ben each pointed a rifle at the man who held her. Jed's rifle was new, but Ben's gun was the old muzzle loader Papa called his "hog rifle." It was used mainly for butchering because each time it was fired, a metal ball and gunpowder had to be tamped into the muzzle before it could be fired again, a process that took several minutes.

"As our guest," Jed said again.

The soldier dropped Valor into the boxwoods.

She tumbled to the ground, scraping her knuckles on the soil and rocks. The soldier leaped the fence and was gone.

"Miss Valor, these Rebs mean. You have to be more careful when they around," said Ben, helping her to her feet.

Jed said, "Val, Uncle John left me in charge. You'll have to do as I say. I have to keep you safe."

"This is my pa's farm," said Valor. "I'm in charge." Her heart was pounding and her breath felt caught in her throat.

"You're a girl," said Jed. "You can't be in charge."

Valor turned away so Jed could not see her hands shake as she grasped her shoulder where Papa's medal reminded her that she must have courage. But touching the medal did not stop the trembling, nor did it stop the terror she felt rising to choke her since the dirty man had grabbed her. She shook herself as if to shake away the filth. She would be in charge, no matter what Jed said.

Valor soothed her bruised hand with the other hand. Then she turned and slammed her fist into the porch pillar.

"I will be in charge, and, Jed, the next time you act like you own this farm, I'll . . ." she said. But Jed had already disappeared around the corner.

She sat down on the top step. Tears burned her eyes. *I will pay you back, you filthy scum. If Jed thinks he is in charge here, why doesn't he do something? I'll show you, Jed. I am not helpless. I will pay you back, all you filthy soldiers. I will become a soldier too!*

CHAPTER 8
(1864)

The war seemed to go on forever. Papa's latest letter had been dated 1864. He wrote of places called Spotsylvania and Cold Harbor. The war was not going well for John McAimee's troops, and his men suffered from lack of food, clothing and weapons.

The long days of the summer had been brightened by the hope that Papa would come home, but those hopes had been dashed by word that the South's hopes of winning the war grew less each day. But war or no war, Savannah said, the crops had to be made if they wanted to eat. So everyone except Sarah, sitting lost to the world in her bed, had helped in the fields. The hot summer sun beamed down on Valor's sunbonnet. Savannah hoed the row of corn ahead of her. Valor stopped, took off her bonnet, and fanned her face with its brim.

"Miss Valor, you put that bonnet back on your head this minute," scolded Savannah. "It's bad enough you out here working like a field hand in this sun. You has to work so we won't starve, but you don't keep that bonnet on, you gonna look like that white trash down at Elsie . . ."

"Oh, Savannah, it's so hot. It's cooler without the bonnet," moaned Valor. Shep lay snoozing in the shade of a lilac bush near the edge of the cornfield.

"I done told your poor, sick mammy that I see to it you gonna grow up to be a lady. You can't be a lady with skin like a field hand," said Savannah. "And . . ."

"Who's riding up this way?" interrupted Valor, looking into the sun as Shep began to bark. "Where is the livestock, Jed?"

"It be some kind of soldier," said Savannah. "He wearing blue or gray? If it be blue, we have to help Ben get the cows and horses off into the woods."

"It appears to be gray," said Valor. Jed had dropped his hoe and moved quietly into the woods out of sight.

"Lordy, one of the home boys. Then the livestock be safe," said Savannah. "Wonder what he wants."

The figure turned off the road, and carefully walked his horse among the new green stalks now just about knee high.

"Howdy, ma'am," the soldier said.

"Howdy," said Savannah. "What you be doing on our land?"

"Well, now, I don't need to explain myself to no slaves," said the soldier, spitting tobacco at Savannah's feet.

Out of the corner of her eye Valor saw Jed level his rifle at the soldier's back from his hiding place in the laurel thicket that bordered the cornfield.

"Sir, this woman be my slave," said Jed in a voice that sounded bigger to Valor than Jed was. "And the lady be my cousin. I would be much obliged if you would address them both as ladies."

The soldier slowly turned around to see Ben join Jed, his rifle also pointed.

"I ain't no soldier. Just took these clothes off'n a dead boy back there after mine was stole. I'm hunting a slave called Donsey what done run off from her master down Rutherfordton way. She took her child and a baby. They's a high price on her head." He grinned down at Valor. She turned so her face was hidden by her bonnet.

"I been told they's a farm summers around here

that hides them slaves what runs away from their masters. You wouldn't be knowing anything about that, now, would you?'' he asked now leering at Valor.

''As a slave owner myself, do you think I'd do anything to help a runaway?'' said Jed, still leveling his gun at the man.

''You never can tell these days,'' said the man. ''I have it on good authority that slaves is being hid by somebody hereabouts. It might well be you'uns.'' He spat at Savannah's feet.

''I'll thank you to be on your way off my land for that insult, sir,'' said Jed.

The man turned his horse and rode slowly away, being careful to step on as many of the young corn plants as he could.

''Filthy white trash,'' said Savannah, following the horse and uprighting the corn plants with her hoe as she went. Jed and Ben walked out of the thicket, their rifles still in their hands.

''Jed, how come you told them that I be your slave?'' asked Savannah. ''You know me and Ben free, and your pappy ain't ever never owned no slaves.''

''Savannah, that man's a bounty hunter. He fights on both sides. The only way to protect you was to let him think you're mine. He never got close enough to see I ain't old enough to be the master yet,'' said Jed.

''Well, Jed, you keep changing sides, and I don't know which side you're on today,'' said Valor.

''I'm on whichever side will protect this farm until Uncle John and Pa get home, or until I'm old enough to join up myself,'' said Jed. ''And I'll be twelve next year.''

''I know, Jed. You are *one* year younger than I am,'' said Valor, her fists on her hips. Jed had grown taller than she was since last spring. ''But how come those men are hunting slaves? Uncle Joe wrote that Mr. Lincoln freed all the slaves.''

Jed stepped toward Valor. She could barely see his eyes under her father's broad-brimmed farm hat. ''Slave owners in the South don't see that President Lincoln has any right to free their slaves. He isn't president of the South. Jeff Davis is. My papa says they are wrong, but they don't think so,'' he said.

Valor looked up at her cousin and saw his brown eyes spark fire in the sunlight. ''I believe you,'' she grinned at him. Then she stood on tiptoe to hug his skinny shoulders. Savannah interrupted the pair.

''It's time to fix your ma some dinner, I guess. Miss Valor, you finish this row and then come on up to the house. We done about all we can this morning."

Savannah leaned on her hoe as she walked toward the house.

"Vallie, we have to do something," said Jed as soon as Savannah was out of earshot.

"Jed, no one's about. Why are you whispering like that?"

"Vallie, we have to go warn the English family before nightfall," said Jed.

"Warn the English family about what?" asked Valor.

"The English family hides runaway slaves and deserters on their farm," said Jed. "We have to warn them about the bounty hunter."

"You mean Isaac English, down by the river bend? He goes hunting with my pa," said Valor, her eyes widening with fear. "You mean they're not loyal to the cause?"

"Depends on what cause you're talking about," said Jed.

"I mean the cause of the South," said Valor. "The cause my pa and one of my brothers are fighting for."

"And I mean the cause that *my* pa and the other of your brothers are fighting for. The preservation of the union of this United States of America," said Jed.

"Jed Burl," said Valor. "You are a traitor."

"Val, your pa knows where my pa stands. They're fighting on opposite sides of the war, but they're still brothers-in-law. And your brothers are fighting on both sides!"

"I'm loyal to the cause my pa's loyal to," said Valor.

"Val, I need your help. You gonna help me or not?"

"Will you take me hunting afterwards?" asked Valor.

"I'll take you hunting first chance I get," promised Jed.

"Then I'll help you tonight. Do you think we could slip off before sundown?" asked Valor. "I can wear Papa's britches. I can pretend . . ."

"Not before this field of corn gets hoed," interrupted Jed. "We'll have to work hard so we can finish. Sav ain't gonna let you work in the high heat of the day, no matter what you tell her. You might as well plan on staying inside until it gets cooler. We don't want to ruin your pretty skin, do we, cousin?" Jed teased.

Valor picked up the hoe and chased him across the field.

"Don't ever chase a man who's carrying a gun," called Jed over his shoulder.

"Man? What man? I don't see a man? I'm chasing *you*, cousin," called Valor.

CHAPTER 9

"We'll have to walk the horses quietly down the east road," said Valor, adjusting the rifle across the pommel of her saddle. "Why do I have to carry this old hog rifle? You can't hit the side of a barn with this gun. Why do you get the best gun?" she asked.

"Because it is my duty to protect you, Aunt Sarah, Savannah and Ben," said Jed. "I need the only good rifle on the place. But tonight nobody would guess you're a girl." Jed laughed. "My cousin, Valiant. You make a right good boy."

Valor stood up in the stirrups and pulled the slouch hat down over her ears. She began to whistle her favorite tune. Sam broke into a canter. Jed pushed Charlotte to catch up with her.

"Do you think Savannah heard us, Jed?" asked Valor, looking over her shoulder.

"She was already snoring when I came down the back stairs," he answered. "She was some tired from all that hoeing corn."

"I would feel better if Shep was along," said Valor. "He could bark to warn us if renegades are about."

"That might be dangerous, Val," said Jed. "We need to be silent tonight. It would help if you could be quiet now." Valor reined Sam to a walk. The plop of the horses' hooves was muffled by the pine needles that carpeted the River Road. Yard dogs began to bark as they passed the big white house at the Fayette Wiseman place, but only the full moon noted the two figures as they forded the river on the trail to the English farm. Jed led the way into the shoals, where a stream of water barely trickled over the rocks.

Suddenly, he reined Charlotte in. He lifted one hand to stop Valor. "Shhh," he whispered.

In the moonlight, Valor could make out a canoe gliding almost soundlessly across the river upstream. A wail pierced the heavy night air only to be stopped abruptly.

"That's a baby's cry," said Valor. She could make out four figures silhouetted against the moon. Two of them wore hats, a third was a woman, and a fourth one was much smaller. Valor pulled in Sam's reins to shrink farther into the shadows of the willows bending down to meet the water.

"They'll see you," she said. "Move back." Jed pulled Charlotte into the laurel thicket. The canoe glided to the far shore. Once it was tied to the bushes, the taller of the two figures wearing hats helped the smaller figures up the bank.

Then the party moved single file along the water's edge. The figures wearing hats leaned over to part the branches of a huge willow tree. The smaller figures seemed to disappear into the branches.

Quickly, two of the figures moved back to the canoe and quietly paddled upstream.

"We have to hurry. That was a baby," said Valor.

"Val," said Jed in a hoarse whisper, ignoring her concern, "we're going hunting with Josiah. Any hurry on our part might get the whole family shot."

"Those bounty hunters may be watching us," she said. "But we have to make sure they don't find that baby."

"Best way's to go about our business," said Jed, his voice growing louder. "Val, you keep up this talking, you're going to scare all the game away. I knew you were too young of a boy to take hunting."

Jed turned his horse away and forded the river. Then he turned and spat into the water.

"I told my maw her baby boy couldn't take hunting," he hissed loudly. "Follow me, Cousin Valiant," he whispered guiding Charlotte through the shoals.

"Jedediah!" said Valor. "I'll thank you to stop spitting at me! I'll . . ."

Without turning his head, Jed said in a voice Valor could hardly hear, "You'll get a move on. I hear horses up on the road."

Valor gave the reins a tug, and Sam stepped one hoof into the water. When they reached the far bank of the river, Valor looked back and saw that the two men sat looking across at the spot where they had hidden a few moments ago.

"Move," she whispered and led the way up the trail to a house where one light shone in the parlor window of the English family.

The pair reined in their horses and dismounted. Valor quickly stepped out of the stirrups.

"Easy, Val. We're here to go hunting," said Jed, slapping her on the shoulder as if she were a boy.

But Valor stuck her hand in her suspenders and swaggered up the front steps ahead of Jed.

"Cousin, we'll never get any hunting done we don't get moving. That moon's high already," she said loudly.

"All right, Cousin," said Jed, trying to overtake her. But Valor had already knocked at the front door. She was enjoying her role and pretending she was a brave man used up some of the energy created by her heart beating fast from fear.

Mr. English opened the door, holding a candle high to see who his visitors were.

"Mr. English, Jed Burl, Joe's son," said Jed. "My cousin, Valiant McAimee, and I've come to see if Josiah can go hunting with us this night. Could we come in, sir?"

"Jed, my boy, you're a sight for sore eyes. Josiah ain't said nothing about a hunting trip, and it's a mite late to be visiting, and now, who is this boy here? Don't recollect no Valiant, but . . ."

Valor interrupted him. "Please, sir, may we come in?" she said frantically. "We *have* to come in. Now."

"Why, young man, what's wrong?" said Mr. English, lifting the candle to look at Valor's face more closely.

"We *have* to come inside," she repeated.

104

"Yes, sir. We do," said Jed.

"Well, come in by the fire and rest a spell," said Mr. English, leading them into the hallway, calling, "Marthy! Marthy!"

Valor and Jed set their rifles inside the hallway by the door and followed him down the long hallway. A tiny lady came out to meet them. Valor started to speak, but Jed clasped her arm. She bit her lip.

"Mr. English, sir. Bounty hunter searching for runaway slaves stopped by my uncle John's farm tonight. He was headed this way. You might be on the lookout for him."

Mr. English met Jed's gaze. Mrs. English stiffened. "We'll do that, my boy. We'll do that. Mighty obliged to you," said Mr. English, rubbing his hands together and shaking his head. "Now, won't you have some cider while I fetch Josiah? Marthy, get these young men a mug of cider, won't you, my dear?"

As he spoke, Mr. English gathered his hat and his rifle. Before Mrs. English could answer, he was down the hallway and out the door. Mrs. English showed them into the parlor and left to get the cider. Valor reached up to take off Ben's old hat. *Better keep your hat on,* she thought. *Better have bad manners than have my hair fall down.*

Valor moved closer to the fire, still wearing her hat.

"Fire feels good," she said, holding her hands toward it.

"Val," barked Jed. "That looks like a girl. Here, stand like this."

He turned his back to the fire, spread his boots far apart, clasped his hands behind him, and rocked back and forth. Heel to toe. Toe to heel.

"You can't make like you're a boy and stand like a girl. Folks'll catch on," he said.

Valor imitated him. Then she swaggered across the sand-scrubbed floor, thumbs laced under suspenders until they both laughed out loud.

"You boys ain't getting boisterous in my parlor, now, are you?" scolded Mrs. English, carrying two mugs through the door. She set the mugs down on the table, lifted the hot poker, and stuck it into the fire. When it glowed red, she stuck it first into one cider cup, then the other. Finally, she handed a mug to each of them.

Valor took a swallow. It burned her throat. She gasped. Jed looked at her and shook his head. She swallowed. Her eyes stung, but she did not cry out.

"Whose boy are you? Did you say it is Valiant?" inquired Mrs. English. "I recollect John's wife had a brother with two or three boys. You one of them?"

Jed answered for Valor. "No, ma'am. He's from down the country. Near Morganton. One of Aunt Sarah's kin. His pa's gone away to the war."

"Well, whatever," she said, settling into her rocking chair and picking up her mending. "You're a mite too pretty to be a proper boy, but I guess you'll outgrow that. Hope this war's over soon, before the young'uns your age have to go. Josiah's all we've got left. He's my baby, and . . ." Mr. English came quietly back into the room.

"Josiah'll be with you. He's saddling up now. Said to meet him at the ford. Soon as you finish that cider."

Jed and Valor emptied their cups.

"Good night, Mrs. English," said Jed. "Much obliged for the cider." He tipped his hat.

"Yes, much obliged," said Valor, tipping her hat quickly, then pulling it down over her eyes.

Mr. and Mrs. English followed the pair and stood on the porch until they galloped away.

CHAPTER 10

They waited at the ford. Soon the clip-clop of hooves signaled Josiah's arrival. He greeted Jed with a slap on the back.

"Who's this?" Josiah asked.

"Cousin Valiant," answered Jed.

Josiah held out his hand. Valor took it firmly.

"Pleased to make your acquaintance," she said softly.

"What are we after tonight? You didn't bring dogs so it can't be 'coon nor fox," said Josiah.

"Heard they's bear sign down by the river," said Jed.

"Might be," said Josiah. "I thought you might bring that pretty little cousin, Valor, with you." He cuffed John's shoulder in the moonlight.

Valor pulled her horse closer to Jed's.

"Jed, I need to stop for a few minutes," she whispered.

"Valiant!" said Jed. "Stay close to the river bank then. We'll wait here." He winked at Josiah. "First hunting trip," he said.

Valor led Sam into the laurel thicket and dismounted. As she pulled her suspenders back over her shoulders, she heard voices. She peered through the leaves. The bounty hunters were talking to Jed and Josiah. She stepped back. Her foot slipped. Suddenly, there was nothing under her feet but air. She felt a cold draft. Then she landed with a PLOP! into the mud.

It was pitch dark, but she could feel the wet murkiness beneath her. She could smell the moldy earth around her. Picking herself up she brushed at the mud that clung to her clothing. Her cap was caught in her hair. She pushed it back over her curls and tucked in her braid. As her eyes grew accustomed to the darkness, she could see the rocks above her head.

The light of the full moon cast her shadow and those of the willow branches behind her on a pile of rocks at her side.

The rocks moved. Valor could see two eyes. She gasped and stepped back. The moonlight fell on a figure, a brown woman, nursing a baby at her breast. Another child peered around her shoulder.

"Lordy, Lordy," whispered Valor. The woman neither blinked nor spoke. She and the child sat as still as stones.

"Oh, dear Lord," said Valor. "You're the ones, Donsey." The woman sat silent, still unmoving. "Oh, you poor thing," whispered Valor. "I won't hurt you. My cousin and I came to warn the people who are helping you that bounty hunters were on the way."

Valor reached out her hand to touch the baby's face. The woman pulled back.

"Please, sir," the woman whispered.

Valor was startled. Then she remembered her clothing. She stepped away.

"I won't hurt you. Do not fear," said Valor.

Shouts and men's loud voices came from the hill above. "That cousin of mine," Valor heard Jed's voice say, more loudly than usual. "Lost again. There's his horse."

"She's been running," said Josiah. "Valiant must have been racing her down the road again. Pa's warned him about that. He slips away nights after everybody's asleep."

"Sure would be obliged if you fellows would keep an eye out for a young boy about so high. He'll

110

be on foot," Jed laughed nervously. "He'll be somewhere downstream. Lost."

The sounds of horses' hooves splashed as the men made their way down the edge of the river. Valor held her breath as they passed by the mouth of the cave, so close that she could have reached out to touch the horse's leg if she leaned forward. Her scalp prickled under Ben's old hat. The voices grew faint, then drifted away.

Valor sat down beside the woman. As the moonlight grew dim toward morning, the small child crept around and climbed up on Valor's lap. He put his head against her shoulder near the place where she wore Papa's medal pinned to her shift. Soon both of them slept.

CHAPTER 11

The sun shone into Valor's eyes. She lifted her head. On her lap, the small child slept, his face hidden against her sweater. The woman sitting beside her stayed perfectly still, her eyes staring straight ahead. The baby's head was snuggled against the woman's bare breast.

"Ma'am," said Valor, trying to stretch her shoulders without disturbing the child. The lady raised one finger to her lips. "Shhh," she said, pointing to the opening of the cave.

Through the willow branches, Valor could see a skiff with three men being poled upstream. Valor froze, hardly daring to breathe. She could feel the fear rising in her throat. She closed her eyes, but when she imagined a sneering face with a red beard, she opened them again.

She continued to sit silently until the sun had

moved across the sky so that the shadow of the riverbank above the cave darkened the space inside. Her legs were asleep, and her arms ached from the weight of the child. Carefully, she moved his weight from one arm to the other, then looked at his face to see if he was all right.

Finally, she heard a familiar voice, "Val! Vallie!" It was Jed.

Valor looked at the woman, who smiled and nodded. Gently, she placed the child on a pile of leaves beside his mother and took a step. Her legs were numb. She fell into the mud at the mouth of the cave again.

"Jed, I'm here," Valor called.

Clods of dirt rained down as Jed made his way through the brush and down to the cave's entrance. He carried a haversack over his shoulder.

"Valor?" he said, peering into the gloom. "How did you find the cave?"

"I fell in," she said, looking up to where he stood on the bank. "And if I had come out, those men would have found them."

She pointed back into the cave where the woman and her children sat. Jed made his way down to the mouth of the cave and handed the haversack to Valor.

"Mrs. English sent some food," said Jed. Suddenly she realized that she was starved. She opened the sack. The aroma of cold fried ham and apple pie made her mouth water. She grabbed for a fried apple pie. Jed leaned back into the gloom of the cave. Valor took a bite, then reached into the sack. She handed the ham biscuit to the young mother who stuffed it whole into her mouth. ''She is starving,'' thought Valor.

''Mr. English says to tell you he has some forged papers that'll be here by nightfall, Donsey. He'll come with the team and wagon about moonrise to get you. Says for you and the young'uns to stay quiet for today,'' said Jed.

The child stirred in his sleep and began to whimper. ''Hungry,'' he whined.

Valor handed the pie to him and gave the sack to the woman. A broad smile brightened Donsey's face.

''Much obliged, sir,'' she said.

''Jed, could we bring her some clean water to drink, and mayhap wash her face?'' asked Valor.

''Josiah's bringing water and yarb tea down from the house,'' he said, and reached out his hand to help Valor climb the steep slope to the road. ''Savannah's gonna be whopping mad we ain't been home yet. Come on,'' said Jed.

Valor took his hand and turned to smile and wave

at Donsey and the children. On the road Sam waited, nibbling the birch branches. She moved quickly to nuzzle Valor's mud-caked face. The pair mounted and began their journey up the river road.

"How did you find me?" Valor asked finally.

"Josiah figured you might have fallen into the cave when you didn't come back. He had seen you go that way. We dursen't come hunt you after the bounty hunters showed up. It would have given away Donsey's hiding place for sure," he answered.

"It's fearsome!" said Valor. "So damp and cold. That poor woman and her children. I fear something's wrong with them. They slept so long. The little boy didn't even waken when I put him down."

"Yarb tea makes the young'uns sleep until they're safe," he said.

"Is that what makes them sleep so much?" asked Valor.

"Josiah says his ma's the best yarb doctor in this valley. She learned from the old witch-woman up river. She knows what yarbs and leaves to mix that'll make a person sleep like death. When a runaway takes her young'uns, they drug them with yarbs so they won't make a noise."

"I'd like to know what leaves and yarbs she gathers. We could give some to Savannah when we want to slip out hunting," said Valor. Jed laughed.

"Mrs. English sent Aunt Sarah some of her mixture right in this poke," he said, lifting a cloth bag tied to the pommel of his saddle. "Last time she came calling, Aunt Sarah said she wasn't sleeping."

"Good," said Valor, with a wink. "Let's stash some away in the corncrib before we give it to Savannah."

"Right after I throw you into the watering trough. You look more like a mud dauber than a boy right now. And a body'd never guess a girl was hiding underneath that cake of mud." Jed laughed.

Valor looked at her hands. They were black with the river mud. Silt formed a fine dust on her pants, and her boots were heavy with peat clinging about her ankles. She could smell the dank, musty river on her skin.

"Yes, we'd better be getting on home," she agreed. "Jed, do you think they'll find Donsey and her young'uns?"

"Not likely," he said. "That cave's a good hiding place, right at the water's edge all covered by the willow withes. Dogs can't track them when they come in by skiff or canoe. They can step right out of a canoe into the cave. That's what fooled the bounty hunters."

"Where are they? I saw them this morning," said Valor.

"Gone back downstream. They lost track of Donsey down on the South Toe River. Followed a tale told by a farmer about a slave he'd seen in a canoe. Give up and headed back by now, I'd guess," said Jed.

"Are Donsey and the young'uns safe?" asked Valor.

"Mr. English's led many a runaway across the Yeller Mountain Trail to freedom. I'll reckon Donsey'll make it," said Jed.

CHAPTER 12

"Valor McAimee!" said Savannah, standing with a fist resting on each hip as the pair rode into the side yard. "Where have you been? Crawling on the bottom of the river?" Valor dismounted and handed the reins to Jed.

"I'll tend the horses. You clean up," he said.

"Lordy, Lordy, child! What happened? You come up on this porch and take off them clothes right now." Savannah walked down the steps to the wash pot near the well house. Lifting the heavy iron pot up to the tripod, she stirred the smoldering ashes underneath it.

Valor removed her mud-caked boots and britches and stood in her drawers and shift. Unpinning Papa's medal, she placed it carefully on Savannah's shelf near the wash pot. Then she took off her cap and unbraided her hair. Brown curls fell about her shoulders, framing a face streaked with red clay and black mud.

Savannah came around the corner of the kitchen porch. Shep ran around the corner and almost knocked Valor down jumping on her.

"Just maybe you can tell me why you wearing Master John's britches and traipsing about the countryside all night a-trying to be a man!" Savannah said, pouring water from the wooden pails she carried from the well into the washpot.

"We went hunting, and I fell into a hole," said Valor. "And I'm so hungry, Savannah. Could I have something to eat?"

"You'll eat when you're clean, and when I have the truth out of you," said Savannah angrily, coming back from the clothesline. She handed Valor a sheet. "Here, wrap yourself in this and come over here," said Savannah.

The sheet bound her ankles so Valor shuffled along the granite slab to the washtub. The spring wind chilled her shoulders. Savannah lifted the iron kettle to pour warm water into the tub. Valor stepped in. Savannah handed her a cake of white lye soap and a heavy square cloth.

"Clean yourself up, young lady, and wash that hair, too," she said, disappearing into the kitchen.

Valor slid down into the warm water. She closed

her eyes. She could see Donsey with her eyes wide like a frightened animal, and the two children in that dark, damp cave. Tears slipped down her cheeks into the soapsuds. She could imagine the terror Donsey felt hiding in the cave. Her own throat constricted. She slipped further into the warm water until her own terror passed.

"Dear Lord," she prayed softly, "please keep Donsey and her young'uns safe. Let her get all the way north. Keep her safe from the bounty hunters. Please do this, Lord, and I'll remember to be good."

She opened her eyes and looked up at the blue sky. A raven winged its way across the white clouds on its way north. "Just like that raven, dear Lord," she added. "All the way north to freedom. I guess Donsey is a sister to the wind too, even if she doesn't wear britches. She had to risk her and her young'uns for their freedom. That takes real courage too. Amen."

"Honey, why don't you tell me about Donsey and her young'uns," said Savannah who was standing by the washtub behind Valor. She pulled up a stool and sat down. She carried a big bowl of creesy greens seasoned with sidemeat in one hand. On the side of the bowl balanced a chunk of cornbread.

"First creesy greens of the season. Ben found

them down in the meadow,'' said Savannah. ''Been cooking all morning. They ought to taste right good.''

Valor opened her mouth to let Savannah feed her just as she had when she was a little child. She was so hungry that the creesy greens and cornbread tasted better than any food Valor had ever tasted before.

''You won't let anyone know, will you, Savannah?'' she asked when her story was finished.

''Lordy, no, honey,'' said Savannah. ''This night'll stay right here in Savannah's ear. We got enough troubles already. That was a foolhardy thing to do, Young Missy. But I reckon old Savannah's right glad you took the chance. I'm right proud of my little missy this day.'' Savannah smiled as she set the bowl down on the flagstones and picked up a pitcher of warm water.

''Hold back your head, Miss Valor. I reckon your pa done named you right. Now, we gonna wash that hair.''

Valor leaned her head back. She almost fell asleep as Savannah washed and rubbed her hair dry with a coarse towel.

Finally she crawled between fresh sheets and slept until late the following day. When she awoke, her body was sore and her muscles were stiff.

121

Savannah had left a new embroidered apron with Valor's old brown dress for her to put on. It was made from one of Mama's linen tablecloths, but it was the prettiest one Valor had ever owned. She stood long in front of the mirror admiring herself. Then she went to find Savannah.

"Your ma's been asking about you all this live-long day. I told her you had a touch of the thysic, so you was still asleep. She's mighty concerned about you," said Savannah.

"Why'd you tell her that?" groaned Valor.

"Better have her concerned about the thysic than her gal a-traipsing about the countryside holping runaway slaves. Thysic's cured with yarb tea," said Savannah. "Traipsing around's putting herself in danger to holp a slave-woman. Now, that's another matter."

Valor knocked on her mother's door and peeped through the opening where the door stood slightly ajar. Her mother sat up in bed staring out the window at the mountains in the distance.

"Mama," said Valor.

"Valor." Her mother looked around startled, confused. "Savannah says you're sick. Come, let me look at you."

Valor walked around to the side of the bed.

"Yes, you do look a little peaked. Have Savannah

fix you some pennyrile tea." She smiled. Then she looked out the window again as if Valor did not exist.

"I love you, Mama," said Valor, but her mother seemed not to hear. She kissed her mother's cheek and tiptoed out the door.

Valor went to find Jed. He was in the stables mending harnesses with Ben.

"That tea," he said, nodding his head toward the corncrib. "In the rat trap hanging on the rafters. When we go hunting again, it's ready."

"Tonight?" asked Valor.

"Tonight I sleep, Vallie," said Jed.

Chapter 13
(1865)

The struggle wore on. Battle lines changed. John McAimee's letters grew ever more sorrowful as he wrote of the plight of his men and of their chances of surviving the war. Uncle Joe's letters to Jed were more hopeful of winning the war but almost as desolate about the conditions under which his troops lived. The Appalachian Mountains were filled with deserters from both sides, whose raids on mountain farms, where crops were sparse from the lack of men to work them, brought hunger and deprivation to lands far removed from battle sites.

"Why do we have to dig up this flower bed?" Valor whined one spring day in 1865. "The ground's not even half thawed. It won't be thawed for another month—at least until the first of May."

"Because this our bed of greens," said Savannah.

"They gonna feed us all summer, and next winter they taste mighty fine."

"Why don't we put them in the garden?" said Valor.

"Because here they will be protected by the rock wall, protected from the marauders and soldiers that come through here," said Savannah. "And next fall the sunshine'll keep these mustard greens growing right through first snow."

"Why do I have to do the digging? I'm almost fourteen years old," whined Valor. "I want to ride Sam up to the falls before night."

"Because, with the menfolks away at war, somebody has to." Savannah shook her head sadly. "Seems like this war will never end. Been nigh onto five years now." She stood for a moment looking at Valor. "Why, your pappy won't even know you, a woman full growed. Put that sunbonnet back up so your face won't look like a fieldhand's."

Valor angrily struck at the soil with her hoe.

"Savannah! Savannah!" shouted Jed. "Soldiers coming. Riding hard!"

"Be they gray or blue?" asked Savannah, wiping her hands on her apron. Shep growled, the menacing sound low in his throat.

"Blue," panted Ben, coming into the doorway behind Jed.

"Well," said Savannah. "We've had blue, and we've had gray. We'll do the best we can. Ben, Jed, get the guns. Oh, Lord. The livestock! They's no time to hide them now."

"Soon as we find out what they want, I'll slip out to the barn and hide the stock," said Ben.

"Let us pray that's not what they want," said Savannah. "Where is Shep?"

"He's fastened up in the woodshed," said Valor.

Savannah straightened her kerchief. To Valor, Savannah seemed to grow a foot taller as they marched through the long hallway to the front door and into the house.

Jed and Ben placed the powder horn and shot bags over their shoulders, grabbed their rifles, and walked to the front porch to stand in front of Savannah. They stood the butts of the long rifles beside their boots and waited.

Valor came to stand beside Savannah. She could see the flag with its stars and stripes whipping in the wind over the front line of blue uniforms as they cantered through the north gap and across the long rise to the front porch.

Three of the riders galloped down the hill to the barn.

"Sam," cried Valor. "They'll hurt Sam." She started to jump off the porch.

Savannah grabbed her arm. "They'll hurt you more, Miss Valor. You come back here."

Four of the men left the group and galloped toward the wide steps of the porch. One of them had a red, almost orange beard. At last, Valor's worst nightmare had come true.

"It's Kirk's men!" said Jed. "That no-good renegade. That red beard. He's a mean, ugly . . . he's nothing but an outlaw hiding behind that flag."

Valor froze. It *was* the man who had hurt her mother. There he was, riding again into the yard of the home he *had* destroyed by breaking her mother's mind and heart. Valor gasped. Suddenly, she *was* the tiny frightened child, small and helpless, hiding inside the dark closet. She was frozen with fear.

"It's Kirk's men," Jed repeated. "That no-good . . ."

"Master Jed, watch your mouth," said Savannah. "Miss Valor, be still. Get behind me."

Valor felt her fists form into balls. A knot of terror formed in her throat. "The man with the red beard has come back to hurt us again," she whispered. *What can I do? What can I do?* echoed over and over inside her head.

"These be mean," said Ben. "What we gonna do?"

"What can we do?" said Savannah. "We stands our ground. This be our home." She turned to Valor.

"Miss Valor, you go hide in the linen press, and don't you come out until this riffraff's off the place. Now, git!" Valor reached for Jed's gun. Savannah caught her wrist and held the girl behind her full skirts.

"Sav, I'm going to . . ." wailed Valor.

"Do as I say!" Savannah almost spat the words at Valor. "That hiding place saved your life once. It may do it again."

As the riders reined in their horses at the front gate, Valor opened the door beneath the stairs in the main hall. She pushed back the sheets and crawled over the lowest shelf into the closet. A knot formed in her throat as she breathed the musty smell of the seldom aired storage room. Panic gripped her as she remembered sitting huddled in the corner four years ago watching her mother fall down the stairs. She hesitated, then pulled the door almost closed so that only a crack allowed her to see the figures on the front porch.

The riders came through the gate single file and reined in at the porch steps. Mismatched blue uniforms, stiff with dust and sweat offered little except color to identify the soldiers as belonging to either the North or the South. At the front of the column rode the red-bearded man who had haunted Valor's nightmares for so long. She could see his small eyes, closely set in his long narrow face, his square chin outlined by his beard. Next in line rode an unkempt man with stringy blond hair.

"Boy, where be your folk?" the ugly man with greasy blond hair asked Jed. His little pot of a stomach hung over the pommel of his saddle. His dirty beard was flecked brown with tobacco juice.

"My pa's away," said Jed. "My ma's dead. My aunt's very ill. I'm in charge here. Who are you?"

"We're with Colonel George Kirk, 3rd North Carolina and Tennessee Federal Volunteers," the blond man said.

"Which side your pa *on,* boy?" asked the red-bearded man, spitting his words at Jed. Even sitting in the saddle he was taller than the others. "We hyeard this be a Reb farm. Your pa John McAimee?"

"No, sir, my pa's Joe Burl."

"These be your slaves?" asked Red Beard.

"I be a free woman," said Savannah, her arms folded across her chest, her voice like muffled drums. "*Not* a slave."

130

"Shut up, wench!" The dirty, blond man pulled his horse closer to the porch and pointed his pistol at Savannah's chest. "Colonel Kirk's men do not *talk* to no womern, not a slave womern nohow. We have better things to do with them." As the man opened his mouth, rotten tobacco-stained teeth outlined the dark area beneath his nose.

"Sergeant Bullock!" barked Red Beard. "I am in charge here. I'll decide who I talk to. This one's a handsome wench, big as the side of a barn, though. Which of you boys want her when I get through with her?" He looked around at his cohorts. The three men who sat near the porch all laughed nervously.

"You got any other womern hereabouts?" said Red Beard. "My boys getting restless. Ain't seen a womern since we left Morganton two days ago."

"I get the first shot at her," said the round fat one, his hat blowing off to reveal a bald head shining in the midday sun.

"Corporal West, you and the men scout the rest of the house while I take a little refreshment in the kitchen," said Red Beard. He laughed, low, guttural. Valor could see Savannah's back grow stiff and her head lift. Red Beard looked around the porch. "Why, I recollect this house and this here wench. Some years back, I stopped here. Lost that pretty silk sash one of my gals made for me. Sure prized that sash. You ain't seen a silk sash with some initials 'HGK' on it, now, have you, wench?''

''We ain't seen no silk in these hills since this awful war done started,'' Valor heard Savannah say.

Red Beard stepped out of the stirrups, to the porch, and disappeared around the corner of the house.

Valor remembered the sash, carefully washed and folded into a ball where Savannah had hidden it on the top shelf of the linen press, above the corner where Valor now crouched in the darkness. ''This be kept for the day Master John come home when this awful war be over. This will holp him find the man who hurt Miss Sarah and make her so ailing,'' declared Savannah the day she hid the sash.

Turning back to her peephole between the shelves, Valor watched three men near the porch dismount. A dapper man who sat on Kirk's left took off his hat to fan his face as he climbed the stone steps. The sun gleamed silver on his shiny, slick hair.

''Major Harris, check the upstairs rooms to see if they're any more womern hiding. Anything you find, you can have,'' said Red Beard with a wink, as he walked back around the side of the house. Sergeant Bullock climbed the steps, looking at Savannah with piercing eyes under the broad brim of his hat.

"This one's mine," said Bullock, grinning at Savannah. He took a step toward her.

Ben lifted his rifle slowly up to Bullock's middle. The muzzle almost touched the front of the blue uniform.

"She be my wife, a free woman," said Ben. "You will not touch her."

The rifle shot echoed. A surprised look spread over Bullock's face as a red stain began to run down each of his legs. The others sat on their horses, frozen, staring at Ben.

Valor's eyes widened. She had never seen Ben so much as slap the horses with the reins when he was plowing. Yet he had calmly shot the man who threatened Savannah. She wondered if the war changed everybody it touched.

"He shot my . . ." Bullock fell forward sprawling, his head through the front door.

"Good for you, Ben," whispered Valor. "Now shoot Red Beard for hurting Mama."

But three pistols rang out at almost the same moment. Ben fell backwards, his head hitting the door frame. His body slumped against the wall.

Savannah's back stiffened, but she did not move. Valor bit the back of her hand to keep from crying out, and hot tears of anger stung her eyes. Other pistols were aimed at Savannah as the horses near the porch moved restlessly. Valor grabbed the shelf and closed her eyes. Then she jumped as Red Beard hissed, "We ain't playing games. Harris and West, go bury Bullock. He's finished. Put away your arms, men. He ain't worth it. Make camp over by the smokehouse. You, wench, come with me. I'm hungry."

Several soldiers who were mounted moved their horses back through the gate as Red Beard stepped over Ben, grabbed Savannah by the arm, and pushed her across the porch. He was startled to realize that she stood face to face with him and that her shoulders were as broad as his. Her face was chiseled black stone, unmoving, frozen with rage.

"Food, womern! Where's the kitchen?" He pushed Savannah in front of him.

Valor watched.

Harris and West pulled Bullock's body into the hallway. As soon as Red Beard was out of sight, the two men knelt and began to strip the body. The silver-haired man quickly pulled off the dead man's boots.

"These are better than mine, even if they are a mite big," he said, quickly pulling off his own boots.

The bald man was too busy going through the dead man's pockets to notice. "A penknife and one, two gold coins," he counted.

In the closet only a few feet away, Valor sat quiet and still, biting the back of her hand as tears silently ran down her cheeks. The stench of the men's unwashed bodies several feet away almost overcame her.

"Gold coins?" said Harris moving quickly toward the other man. "I get one of them."

"They're mine. I found them," said the little bald man, dancing up and down first on one foot and then the other.

"We divvy up. Give it to me," said Harris.

"You can have his clothes," said West. "Here, I'll help you."

Beginning to unbutton the dead man's uniform, the dapper silver-haired man seemed to forget the gold coins. The bald man tugged at the dead man's pants.

Through the open front door, Valor could see Jed kneeling on the porch beside Ben's body, weeping soundlessly. The soldiers had not noticed Jed's gun stood leaning against the back of the pillar. Silently and suddenly, he picked up his rifle and, leaping off the porch, disappeared.

Inside the closet, Valor sat without moving, anger and fear tightening her chest.

"Too bad," said Harris leaning down to examine the wound.

135

"To those of you who tolerate Jezebel, I will throw into great tribulation, and I will strike her children dead . . .'' proclaimed West, raising his arms over his head.

"You little banty rooster. This ain't no time to be quoting Scriptures,'' said Harris, walking into the parlor across the hall. "Look what I found!'' he said as he returned holding up a bottle, pulling out the stopper, and taking a long swallow. When he had wiped his lips, he sighed. "Scuppernong wine.''

"Let me have a swig,'' called West.

"When you've shared the gold with me,'' said Harris, hiding the bottle behind him.

The two began to climb the stairs, still arguing, Harris holding the bottle high over his head. West followed, jumping every other step like a small cur jumping for a bone.

Jed tiptoed down the hall. Picking up the dead man's uniform coat and britches, hat and boots where the others had dropped them, he took a red basket from its peg on the wall and opened the door to the linen press a bit wider.

"Val,'' he whispered, not looking down. "I'm going to take these things out to the tack room. I'll bring you Uncle John's riding clothes in the basket.

I'll put it on the top shelf. When everybody's gone, you change into them.''

"Why?" whispered Valor. "I want to help you. I can shoot, and I am strong. I'm coming out now!"

"Val, talk some sense. Only way you'll be safe now is if they think you're a boy. These men will do worse than kill you. We have to keep Aunt Sarah and this family safe. If we kill Kirk, they'll kill us and burn the farm to the ground!''

"Then bring me Mama's scissors, too," she said.

"What for?" asked Jed.

"Never mind, just bring them," she whispered. "Shhh. Somebody's coming."

Jed lifted the basket to his shoulders and walked slowly out the door. Two soldiers came in and dragged Bullock's body down the hallway to the back door, leaving a trail of blood.

"Colonel said for us to bury him," said one.

"I ain't rode hard all day to dig no grave now. We'll just take the seat off the privy and stuff him down in the hole," said the other.

"Won't he stink?"

"Yeah, but we won't be here. Serves him right. He will be where he belongs. Sergeant Bullock always was a . . ."

The voices grew faint, so Valor could not hear

what he said. "Oh, Lordy," she whispered. "They are so mean to each other. What on earth will they do to us?"

A shot rang out. Val jumped. The short fat man tumbled down the stairwell. Harris followed, gun in hand. He knelt on one knee and pulled the gold coins from the dead man's pockets. Then he lifted the bald head to unfasten a gold chain from the man's neck. He opened the locket attached to the chain. "Well, I'll be," he whistled. "Who would have thought it? It's that drummer boy we had at Spencer, the one that deserted." He continued to shake his head as his boots clomped down the front steps.

Valor moved further into the shadows of the closet, shrinking back and pulling her knees close to her chin. She held her knees to stay her feet from moving out of the storage room. Her mind was filled with visions of tearing at Kirk's throat with her bare hands and of using the butt of Jed's rifle to pound that red beard into the dust of the sideyard.

As she looked out of her hiding place, she could see Ben's body lying on the porch. Her rage turned to a sorrow that threatened to choke her. Then the rage tore at her again. She held on to her knees. Through clenched teeth, she whispered, "I will hurt you. I will. For what you did to my mama and to

Ben. I'll hurt you. Just wait and see, Colonel Kirk!''

After a long while, exhaustion overtook Valor and she finally slept, her head resting against the rough boards of the closet wall.

CHAPTER 14

Valor awoke to hear Jed's voice somewhere near her head. She was lying on a pile of rags near the back of the closet.

"Val, I'm putting the basket on the top shelf. I couldn't find your cap, so I brought Ben's old hat to hide your hair. Wait until I come to tell you it's safe to come out after dark."

"Jed, they're killing each other!" said Valor. "What will they do to us? Where's Savannah? Is Mama all right? I have to come out and help you."

"Val, stay where you are," whispered Jed. "Pa says Kirk's renegades would be hanged if it weren't for the war. They're a mean bunch. They do awful things to womenfolk, so you have to stay hid. Kirk still has Savannah locked in the summer kitchen."

"Jed, they killed Ben," said Valor, hot tears of

anger burning her eyes. "He wouldn't hurt a fly."

"I know, Valor, but we can cry when Kirk and his renegades ride off this farm. If we cry now, it may get us killed. Or worse. That goes double for you."

"Jed, you can't let Kirk go free! Look at what they did to Ben and to Mama," said Valor.

"If those renegades find you, no telling what they'll do. Stay back there, Vallie. I'll do what I can, but you have to stay hid!"

"Jed, I'm worried about Mama," argued Valor. "I'm hungry, too."

"I'll check on her," said Jed. "And as soon as I can get into the kitchen, I'll bring you something to eat." His footsteps died away, and the house was quiet.

Valor could hear shouts and singing from the meadow near the barn. Finally she changed into her riding clothes and waited. Then she dozed again. She woke with a start.

"Valor," whispered Jed's voice. "Aunt Sarah is all right. Major Harris is an old friend of hers. She told me he is watching out for her."

"Did you bring the scissors?" asked Valor.

"No, you don't need scissors," said Jed.

"I do need scissors," she hissed.

"Boy, where do you keep the keys to the smoke-house?" asked Red Beard. Jed jumped and slammed the closet door.

"They're in Uncle John's study," said Jed, moving away from the closet as fast as he could. "I'll get them."

Valor listened for a long time. When there were no more sounds in the hallway, she reached through the shelves and opened the door. She looked out through the stacks of sheets. No one was in sight. She pulled the sheets off the lowest shelf back into the darkness and slithered out to the hall. She reached back for her boots and Ben's hat. Then she pulled the stack of sheets into place again.

Tiptoeing down the hall to her mother's room, she quietly opened the door. In the twilight she could see the outline of her mother's face against the open window.

"Mama," she whispered.

"Valor Matilda," her mother answered. Finally, she looked around at her daughter. "You are a lady. What on earth do you mean wearing your father's trousers?"

Valor realized that her mother had no idea of what was going on. Some days her mind seemed to be in another world.

"Savannah told Jed to have me dress this way. If

those men find out I'm a girl, they may hurt me,'' she tried to explain.

"You are a lady," Sarah repeated. "Where is Savannah? I'll have a word with her for this." Her mother behaved as if nothing had happened.

Valor had to make her mother understand how dangerous their situation was. She grasped her mother's shoulders and spoke slowly as if to a child. "Mama, we are in danger. Some soldiers are here. Mama, Jed says Kirk is locked in the kitchen with Savannah," said Valor. "I'm afraid he might hurt her. He said she was his."

"Oh, my lord," said Sarah. Her eyes finally focused on Valor's face.

"Mama, do you know they kill each other, and then they steal things from the bodies? Mama, I'm afraid of them."

"You are a lady, Valor," insisted Sarah. "Charlie Harris would never hurt a lady."

"Where are your scissors, Mama?" Valor would just have to take matters into her own hands. Her mother did not seem to comprehend anything.

"In my mending basket by the bed," said Mama. "But please be careful. Charlie was an old beau of mine in Raleigh before I met your father. He will watch out for you."

Valor spoke slowly, deliberately. "I am fearful,

Mama. I saw Major Harris kill his friend and take his chain and his gold coins," said Valor. "Where *are* your scissors?"

Valor found the scissors in the embroidery basket and walked to Mama's dresser. She took the mirror from the hook and carried it to the chair near the window. She leaned the mirror on the back of the chair and took a lock of her hair.

As she snipped at the brown braids, Mama's voice said softly, "Is it that bad, my child?" Mama seemed to be coming back to reality.

"I am fearful, Mama," said Valor, turning to face her mother.

"Then come here, child, and let me cut it for you," said her mother sadly. "Tell me what has happened."

Valor sat on the floor beside the bed while Mama cut her braids into a cap of ringlets that framed her face. Valor sat very still, then her shoulders began to shake.

"Mama, they shot Ben. He's dead. They shot him," said Valor, crying softly.

"Poor old Ben," said Mama. She seemed as unaffected as if Valor had asked for a drink of water. "Where is Savannah?"

Valor said again, "Mama, Ben's *dead.*"

Her mother continued to stare at her, uncomprehending, as she said, "He was a good man." Her mother's face was blank. "Where is Savannah?" she repeated.

"I don't know. I'm afraid Kirk will hurt her. He has her locked in the summer kitchen, Jed says."

"Where were you while this was going on?" asked Miss Sarah.

"I hid in the storage room under the stairs. Mama, *I saw them kill two of their own men.*" Valor shuddered, but her mother's eyes seemed unfocused.

"Oh, you poor child." She stroked Valor's hair and face. "How frightful for you! Yes, you must stay hidden. Major Harris says they will leave by morning."

"Mama, is Major Harris the silver-haired one?"

"Yes, he is quite handsome," said Mama. She seemed to be fading into another time again, her mind not comprehending the reality of the situation. "The girls in Raleigh used to call him a silver-tongued devil, too." Sarah giggled, her blue eyes clouding again. "He was quite a ladies' man."

Valor had to make her mother understand the danger. Grasping both her mother's shoulders she shook her, and spoke deliberately. "Mama, stop it! Major Harris helped kill Ben, and then he killed his friend and stole a locket and chain from him. Mama,

145

please, stop it! I need you here to help us. I need you, Mama.''

Sarah's eyes widened. She sat quietly, her hands folded. She appeared to wake up more fully.

''Charles? Killed his friend? Then he might try to harm you, my Valor,'' she said, shocked. Her eyes narrowed and her jaw clenched.

Then Sarah firmly pushed the covers back and swung her feet off the bed. As if she had never been sick, she stood by the bed, holding onto the bed-post. For the first time in four years, Valor saw her mother's eyes look as if she were truly alive. Finally, her mother said, ''Valor, look in the top drawer of your father's bureau. Bring me the pistol.''

Valor brought the pistol to her mother, who stuck it under the mattress between the straw tick and the feather bed where she lay.

''My child, take off that shirt,'' said Sarah.

''Why?'' asked Valor.

''We must bind your bosoms. Yes, we must make sure that Major Harris and the others never know you are female. Bring me a binding cloth from the bureau,'' she said.

Valor held her arms high so her mother could wrap her chest tightly and tuck the ends of the cloth strip under her shoulder blades.

"Put on the shirt," said Sarah. "Yes, that will do. Now stand with your knees apart. Fine. I've always worried so that you behaved so much like a boy. Now it may save your life and your virtue, too."

There were steps on the stairs.

"That will be Charles," said Sarah. "Vallie, no matter what I do or how strange it seems, do not make a sound. Not one sound. Here, under the bed. Hurry." Picking up her boots, Valor quickly crawled as far under the bed as she could.

Sarah's hand reached down to scoop up the brown curls from the rug. Then she leaned over the chamber pot and lifted the lid. As she replaced it, Harris opened the door.

"Sarah, my dear. I came back as I said I would," he said softly.

The man swayed slightly. Valor could see Mama's crystal wine decanter in one hand and a candlestick in the other. He put the candlestick on the table beside the bed.

"Charles, my dear man. Do come in," Sarah whispered.

"You know, Sarah, we should have married," said Harris. "What made you leave me for this farmer?"

147

"Charles, my life is filled with regrets. If you'll allow me, I'll make amends." She reached out her arms to him.

Anger choked Valor. What was her mother doing? She wanted to ask how on earth she could do such a thing, but she kept still, hardly daring to breathe. "For old time's sake, huh, Sarah? Your man will never know," said Harris, as he took off his jacket. Then he sat on the side of the bed to remove his boots. Sarah put her arms around his neck and kissed his cheek where the silver hair fell over his shoulders.

"For old time's sake," he repeated.

Valor closed her eyes. Then she heard the man kiss her mother. Both his boots disappeared. Valor felt rage fill her throat, but she lay perfectly still. Somehow she sensed that her mother was playing some kind of game Valor did not understand. "No matter what I do or how strange it seems, do not make a sound," her mother had told her.

"Yes, Charles, for old time's sake. For Janette's sake and for all the others," said Sarah, her voice growing cold.

The straw tick above Valor's head moved. Then she saw her mother's hand reach down beside the bed and pull the pistol from its hiding place and disappear from sight.

The pistol cracked. Valor jumped.

"Sarah," the man whispered. "What? Why have you shot me?" His silver hair hit the rug first.

"For Janette and all the others you used and tossed away, Charles, and so you cannot hurt my daughter," said her mother's voice. "Vallie, come out and help me."

"Mama, you shot him!" said Valor, scrambling out from her hiding place. "You killed a man!"

"He won't hurt my daughter as he has hurt so many others," said Sarah calmly. "I did what I had to do."

She pushed the man's feet and legs off the bed. Then she threw off the coverlid and stood holding the bedpost. She swayed, but steadied herself. "He is bigger and stronger than both of us. The only way to stop him was to take away that advantage, to get him to lie down."

"Mama," gasped Valor. "You are too weak. Savannah says . . ."

"Valor, help me drag him to the window," her mother commanded. "If he is found here, those men will kill us, too."

Sarah spoke calmly but surely as she moved away from the bed, leaning to lift Harris's shoulders and pull his pants up around his waist. "Valor, grab his belt and help me."

Tugging and pushing, the pair finally managed to push Harris's head over the low window sill.

"I'm sorry you had to see me this way. And to see a man unclothed, but," said Sarah, as she pulled the man's shoulders through the open window, "I couldn't let him hurt you, my baby."

Sarah pushed the man's arms through the window, and his weight pulled him over. They heard him hit the boxwoods below. "Bring me the wash pitcher and towel from the washstand. We have to clean up the blood," she said.

Valor wrung out the towel in the washbowl and wiped the blood from the floor.

"Mama, you are too weak," said Valor.

"Nonsense," said Sarah. "I have my strength back. Work needs doing. We have to do whatever is necessary to survive. This feather bed's ruined. Help me turn it over, Vallie."

Together they turned the feather tick, and Mama fell exhausted across the bed.

"Valor, you have to have a safe place to sleep. Go drag the tick off your bed and put it on the floor. You can sleep here," said her mother. "I have your papa's pistol to protect us."

Valor tiptoed up the stairs, pulled the feather tick off her bed, and dragged it into the corner behind her mother's bed.

Soon Valor was asleep, but her mother only dozed as she watched the door, pistol loaded and ready to fire. Through the windows the campfires flickered in rhythm, it seemed, to the raucous laughter of the renegades. Shep barked loudly from the woodshed.

"In the morning, we'll let him free," said Sarah.

CHAPTER 15

The first rays of sun came through the gap. Valor woke as her mother jumped, startled as the light touched her eyelids. Noises outside grew louder.

Sarah got up and walked to the window. "Valor, come. See. What's happening down there?" she asked.

The soldiers had taken the farm wagon and Sarah's carriage from the barn. The wagon was loaded with the few hams left in the smokehouse and the rest of the potatoes and corn, which would have provided food until the new crops of summer came in.

Behind the wagons, soldiers herded the cattle, the sheep and the team of plowhorses. Tied to the back of the wagon walked Valor's horse, Sam, and Charlotte.

"Sam!" cried Valor. "They are taking Sam!"

"Sam? Who's Sam?" asked Sarah. Valor had told her mother about her filly many times, but she had seemed not to hear. She had only smiled, that far-away look in her eyes, as if Valor were not there.

"She's my horse," said Valor, running toward the door. Her mother grabbed Valor's arm.

"Vallie, come back here," said her mother. "There's nothing you can do."

"But they're taking Sam. They're taking all our livestock," wailed Valor.

"This is war, my child. We're lucky to have our lives," said Sarah. "These men will hurt you. You must remain hidden."

Two of the men finished piling soil on three graves near the barn. Red Beard rode his horse up to the porch.

"You can't take our livestock," pleaded Jed. "We'll starve. We are Union. My father is in the Union army."

"Boy, we take what we need or want. This is war, and according to all accounts, this is a Reb farm. Like as not, you're making up a story about your pa," said the tall red-bearded man. "Besides I left three of my men with you, in the graves on the hill."

Jed was angry. "I'll follow you," he shouted, shaking his fist. "I'll get you."

153

"You'll do what, boy?" sneered Red Beard.

"I'll follow . . ."

"You won't be able to," said the man. Carefully lifting his pistol, he shot Jed's leg just above the knee. Jed fell to the ground.

"Try anything else, and you'll get worse," said the man, spurring his horse. He wheeled his horse around and turned back to say, "You're lucky. If it wasn't for that wench's biscuits and loving, I'd burn you Rebs out. But, don't you worry, Savannah, the next time I'm by this way, I'll be back for more."

Savannah stood as unmoving as a tree, staring at the blue uniform. Then she seemed to come to her senses. She looked at Jed lying on the ground. She bent down. The boy had fainted. Savannah lifted him and cradled him in her arms. Two men rode by the barn and threw a torch through the door. Flames engulfed the gray boards.

"Jed's been shot," said Valor, running out the door and down the stairs.

"Wait. I'm coming," said Sarah. She walked down the stairs, head held high as if she had never been sick a day in her life.

Savannah put Jed to bed on the parlor settee. She nursed the wound and gave him herb tea to make him sleep. Savannah's eyebrows flew up, but she gave no notice that Sarah had come downstairs for

154

the first time in years. Valor followed Savannah to the summer kitchen.

"What are we going to do?" asked Valor. "Why did Mama suddenly get well?"

"I don't know why Miz Sarah get well right now, but thank the Lord she did. As for what we do, first, we're going to slice these taters I had hid in the kitchen and make soup, right now. Then you and me, we gonna dig my Ben a proper grave and bury him Christian," said Savannah.

Tears were streaming down each of her ebony cheeks, but her voice never faltered. Valor, dropping the knife and the potato she was peeling, put her arms around Savannah's waist. The tall black woman began to wail, a high pitched, lonely sound that seared Valor's soul. Then they held each other and cried and rocked back and forth until Savannah's keening subsided.

By sundown, Valor and Savannah had dug a grave in the little cemetery near the back pasture on the rise at the gap. They wrapped Ben's body in a blanket. Then Savannah lifted her husband's frail form and carried it over to the yawning earth.

Valor recited the Twenty-third Psalm. Savannah knelt, her knees in the red earth, her face lifted to heaven. She no longer cried out, but rocked back and forth silently, tears streaming down her face.

Finally, she picked up the shovel and threw soil into the grave. Valor began to push the dirt with her hands. Soon they were finished.

Savannah leaned on the shovel as they walked back to the house. Valor put her arm around Savannah's waist and snuggled her head to her friend's arm.

"Jedediah is awake," said Sarah when they passed the open parlor window.

As Valor fed him a bowl of potato soup, she asked, "Which way did they go?"

"I heard one of them say they were going across the Yeller Mountain to Tennessee. He's in the 3rd Volunteers. Most of that bunch is from Tennessee," said Jed.

"How long will it take?" asked Valor.

"With the cattle, two, three days," said Jed. "They'll probably head up Roaring Creek and cross through the gap. It's the main road. They might cross Double Head, but my guess, it'll be Roaring Creek. Water's down this time of year."

"How will they know which road?" asked Valor.

"It's the main road, even if it's called the Yeller Mountain Trail. Pa and I rode it when I was little. The Henson Creek Road is really a trail."

"Would they be hard to track?" she asked.

"Vallie, even you could track all those horses and

156

cows. The sheep tracks'll be easy to follow. As for the horses, Ben always made the horseshoes with that 'M' on them for Uncle John's horses. That'll be easy to see in the soft dirt. You aiming to follow? That's what I'd do, but you can't. You're a girl."

Jed had finished his soup. Valor stood up. "Where did you say you put that yarb tea Miz English sent to Savannah?" she asked.

"In the rattrap in the corncrib rafters. I don't need any more tea," said Jed.

But Valor was already out the door.

"Where are you going?" Jed called.

"Out," called Valor. "I'll tell you later."

Carefully, she climbed the corncrib wall, sticking the toe of each boot into the cracks formed by the boards Ben had placed to leave room for the air to circulate and dry the corn.

There's no one to do this except me. Ben's dead. Jed's lame. Mama needs Savannah. Without the horses, we can't plow. Then we'll starve, she argued to herself as she climbed down with the sack slung over her shoulder. She closed the door and walked across the barnyard to the smoldering ashes where the barn had been.

"Poor Sam." She stopped suddenly. "Sam! I have to find Sam and bring her back. She is *my* horse! That filthy Colonel Kirk! He stole my Sam."

157

She turned back to the house. There was only one thing for her to do. She would show her papa that she was in charge of the farm while he was away.

"Colonel Kirk, I will find you! I will get my horse. I will bring the livestock home. I will make you pay for what you have done to my family."

The words of the old witch-woman rang in her ears. "I am a sister to the wind!" she said, reaching up to touch her papa's medal. "My name is Valor. And I am a sister to the wind. If I can find Aunt Becky Linkerfelt, she will know just what to do."

Suddenly, the sorrow of the day lifted from her heart. Valor felt brave and strong enough to defend her home. She flung her arms wide, and the breeze ruffled her short hair as she faced the full moon rising over Humpback Mountain.

"I will show you—all of you. I am a sister to the wind."

CHAPTER 16

The waning moon shone into Valor's room as she pulled Ben's hat down over her ears. Pinning Pa's valor medal to the binding cloth that constricted her chest, she buttoned Jed's shirt. Then she checked her haversack again. Inside she had matches and tender, a powder horn and a bag of shot, tamping rags and flint. There was also the small black iron kettle Pa used for hunting trips, and tucked inside was a packet of herb tea.

She had also sneaked Pa's pistol from its place under the featherbed in her mother's room while her mother was helping Savannah care for Jed. In her bag she had pistol balls, too. She stuck the pistol into the top of her trousers.

"Savannah should be asleep in the parlor, taking care of Jed," she told her faint reflection in the hallway mirror.

Quietly, Valor tiptoed down the back stairs by the summer kitchen, carrying her boots and haversack in one hand and Papa's old hog rifle in the other. Jed's good rifle was in the parlor, so she could not get it without waking Jed or Savannah. Quietly, she opened the door of the linen press and felt along the top shelf until her fingers touched the silk of the rolled-up sash that belonged to Red Beard. Valor stuffed the ball inside her haversack.

I will find a way to let him know who followed him and took our livestock back, she vowed.

The night air was cool. She stopped by the tack room and pulled on the heavy sweater Sarah had knitted for Papa before he went to war.

Then she slipped into the summer kitchen. She found a leftover biscuit and one piece of cornbread cake, cold boiled potatoes in the pot, and some strips of dried pumpkin from the few strings left hanging from the kitchen rafters by the soldiers. Stopping by the root cellar, she found one onion head, a few carrots and a few of the last of the Winter John apples. Shep whined from the woodshed door. She stopped for a moment. Shep would be good company, she thought. *No, Mama and Savannah will need him here.*

She set out toward the gap but turned back to look at the pretty house Pa had built for Mama, as it seemed to lie sleeping in the moonlight. Valor looked at the sky. "Oh, Lord," she prayed, "please make me brave as my name. Please take away my fears. Please bring me and the livestock over the mountain home. And please, Lord, help me find the Yeller Mountain Trail. Amen."

Valor took a deep breath, and looking back at the woodshed where Shep barked, she threw the haversack over one shoulder, the rifle over the other, and walked down the ridge to the west. Tree frogs sang from the banks of the river as Valor made her way up the road. Her eyes searched the nearby brush, but she saw nothing in the darkness.

I miss Ben, she thought. A wave of loneliness swept over her. She felt sure if she turned back to the big house, she would find Ben nodding by his cabin fire while Savannah sewed. Then she remembered the grave on the hill where she had helped Savannah shovel the soil over the blanket-covered figure that afternoon. She pulled the silk sash out of her haversack and clenched it in her hands. *I'll find you! I'll hurt you, Kirk! I'll pull every red whisker out of your face. I'll kill you, just like you killed Ben!* She sobbed. Then sadness came in great gulps as tears wet the collar of Papa's sweater. Valor leaned against a tree and wept.

When she could cry no more, she wiped her eyes

on her sleeve and blew her nose on the handkerchief she found in the pocket of Papa's sweater. Overhead a hoot owl called "Who . . . Who . . . o . . . o." Valor thought the owl sounded like Ben calling "Soo . . . Soo . . ." to the cows at milking time.

Finally, her sorrow and anger spent, Valor looked at the moon moving overhead. The night noises were soothing. She had been hunting often enough to recognize most of them. After a while she began to sing softly under her breath, the same song she sang with her papa before he went away to fight in this awful war.

"The gypsy rover came over the hill,
And down through the valley so shady.
He whistled and sang 'til the green wood rang,
And he won the heart of a lady.
Ah dee do. Ah dee do da day.
Ah dee do, ah dee daisy.
He whistled and sang 'til the green wood rang,
And he won the heart of a lady."

The road seemed long as it wound along the top of the ridge. The Collins house was dark, but the yard dogs barked as she passed. At the Wiseman house, a big hound joined her for a ways. Finally, he turned back. As the sky grew pink, then orange over Buck Hill, Valor stopped to eat.

162

When she had finished her biscuit, an apple and some dried pumpkin, she leaned over to drink from the branch. As she started to wash her face, she saw the reflection of a young boy in the water. Her heart leaped to her throat. Startled, she pulled back. The boy was wearing Ben's hat and the face was her own. Valor laughed out loud. She had even fooled herself. Her heart grew lighter.

"Best get a move on, *Val,*" she said aloud.

The road followed the river. The day was unusually warm for April, and soon she stuffed Pa's sweater into her haversack.

Have to remember to walk like a boy, she told herself, taking long steps and swaggering side to side.

A wagon carrying a few sacks of corn on its way to the mill passed her, driven by a man as old and bent as an ivy bush. Valor remembered to tip Ben's hat to the old man.

"Good day, Uncle," she said with a smile. "Going to the mill?"

"Right cocky young feller," said the old man. "Keep that up and you're looking for a fight." He ignored Valor's question and passed her without further comment.

Valor giggled.

I fooled him! I fooled him! she said to herself.

All day she walked, waving occasionally to a

passerby and always remembering to tip Ben's hat. She had to pretend to be only passing the time. If she seemed to hurry, anyone she passed might realize where she was headed and try to stop her. So she sauntered up the road whenever she was in sight of a passerby or whenever she passed a house. Then, when she had the road to herself, she walked as fast as she could.

Despite her casual appearance, inside her head Valor kept repeating, *I'll get you, Kirk! You'd better not hurt my pony! I'm coming after you.* Her anger at the red-bearded man fueled her determination to repay him for all the pain he had caused her family. *I give myself the freedom to be brave. I will show you I am a sister to the wind.*

Her body ached with fatigue and her eyes stung, so she talked to herself to keep up her courage. "If I don't bring the livestock home, we'll all starve next winter! I'll show Jed that I am in charge, even if I am a girl," she repeated aloud.

Finally, the sun set over the Big Yellow Mountain, leaving the sky crimson in the east. The moon rose, its bright light marking the narrow winding road and reflecting from the river. She passed Plumtree Ford and made her way toward the place where Roaring Creek marked the Yellow Mountain Trail's branching from the main road.

In the moonlight she could see a white house with a dark trim around the roof and the front porch. Huge boxwoods almost hid the front door. She had passed the house in Papa's wagon. It was Aunt Becky's house.

"Always ready to lend a helping hand," Papa had said that day. Now Valor repeated his words aloud.

"Maybe she can tell me how to get to the Yeller Mountain Trail," Valor said. "Maybe she can help me find Colonel Kirk and rescue our livestock. And I guess she'll be willing for me to sleep on her porch until daybreak."

Valor opened the wooden gate and tiptoed across the porch, careful not to allow the haversack or the rifle to make a noise against the floor as she set them down. She eased her body into the corner away from the night breeze. A bird called in the distance.

"Mighty early for a whippoorwill," she said as sleep weighed down her eyelids. "I'll only sleep for a few minutes." Valor's head slumped to her chest as she slept.

CHAPTER 17

"What are you doing here, boy?" asked a low voice that sounded like pines soughing in a spring breeze, startling Valor into wakefulness.

Valor opened her eyes. "I'm not a . . ." She stopped herself. It was Aunt Becky, the old wise-woman.

As Valor struggled to her feet, a hand like a claw reached out to help her stand. Valor was now taller than the woman by a head. She stared down at the topknot and the wreath of white flowers woven into it. Should she tell Aunt Becky who she was or wait to see if the old woman recognized her? She decided that if she could fool Aunt Becky, she could fool anybody else.

"I'm just waiting for sunup," said Valor in her lowest voice. "I wanted to ask how to find the

Yeller Mountain Trail. My papa says you are the kindest person alive, so I hoped you could help me.''

''Who be your papa?'' said the voice like a soft song in Valor's ears, asking the important question which members of the Appalachian culture used to establish a stranger's place in one of the area's families or as an outsider. The woman was dressed in a jacket and pants as Valor remembered.

''John McAimee. I'm Va . . .'' she stuttered. ''I'm his son, Valiant.''

The bright blue eyes stared at her.

''You be no kind of a boy,'' said the voice, with a soft laugh. ''Why you tryin' to be?'' The woman stared up into Valor's eyes.

''I *am* Valiant McAimee,'' Valor struggled to stand the way Jed did when he was mad, with her feet apart and her hands on her hips.

''You be no kind of a boy,'' the voice repeated. ''You be familiar, but I can't place you yet. Anyways, you ain't had a bite to eat this morn either, have you?''

''No, ma'am. I've been walking most of the night,'' said Valor.

''Come on in here. I just made a pot of chicory-root tea and a pan of biscuits. Then you can tell me

167

why you air going down this here road all dressed up in men's britches with your hair all cut off short."

"Well, Auntie, I see you wear men's britches, too," growled Valor.

"That's different," said the old woman shaking her head and laughing softly as she motioned for Valor to come through the front door.

Picking up her haversack and the rifle, then checking to find the pistol safe, Valor walked through the front door. She stared at the array of dried flowers and plants lining the walls of the hallway. Pungent fragrances, most of which were new to her, and a growing pain in her stomach made Valor's head swim. She reached out to catch herself with the door frame.

"You be no kind of a boy," the old woman repeated. "Or else you ain't got no kind of raising." She laughed softly again. "Boy with raising would take off his hat in the house."

She walked down the hall and waved for Valor to follow. Quickly removing her hat, Valor made her way into the warm kitchen. As she sat at a small table with a kerosene lamp in the center, the old woman tied an apron around her waist, poured a cup of steaming liquid and offered an earthen crock.

"Sourwood honey," whispered that soft voice,

as she set a pan of biscuits on the table. Valor's mouth watered. "No butter for the biscuits, though. Yankee scum done run off with my milk cow last week. She was due to come fresh, too. Lost a cow and a calf, too. Worst of all, they took my fine horse, Gray, the only one I had left." A clicking sound as she touched her tongue to her lips punctuated the seriousness of the situation for the old lady.

Valor stuffed half a biscuit into her mouth, ignoring the honey crock. She swallowed most of the cup of chicory tea in a gulp. "May I have some more?" she asked.

Silently, the old lady filled her cup again, broke open a biscuit and drizzled honey on it. Then she handed it to Valor. As Valor stuffed it into her mouth, the old lady broke off a piece of biscuit and chewed on it.

"You sure eat like some kind of a boy." The old lady chuckled.

Valor stopped and straightened her back, broke off a piece of biscuit and ate it daintily. Savannah would scold her for weeks if she saw her eating like a field hand.

"See? I said you was no kind of a boy." The old lady chuckled again softly. "Now, suppose you tell

170

me who you be and what you be doing all alone on this big road with a war going on 'round here?"

Valor stared at the dried-apple face and the bright eyes. The woman sat placidly staring back. Waiting.

"Well, I'm really John McAimee's daughter, Valor. Yesterday . . ."

"I knowed you was familiar. We've talked together. You are a spirited little one, now. Ah, yes. You are the little sister to the wind. I do remember you. But, do go on," said the old lady.

"Yesterday Colonel Kirk and some of his men took . . ."

"Filth. Filth. Scum of the earth," the old lady spat the words out. "Renegades. Robbing. Pilfering. Filth. Plain filth. Go on, little Valor. Tell me the rest."

"They came to our house. They killed Ben. They shot Jed in the leg and tried to hurt my mother. They took my horse, Sam . . ." The words came out so fast they all ran together.

"Now, now, now." The old lady held up one claw-like hand. "Little Valor, slow down and tell me exactly what happened."

Valor began her story with the birth of Sam and how she had named him for Sam Blaylock. Finally, she finished in tears as she remembered Ben. The woman handed Valor a clean rag to wipe her eyes.

"So you decided to take Jed's place and go after the stock?" asked the old woman.

"Yes," Valor answered. "I cut my hair so nobody would notice I ain't a boy. But how did you know? Don't I look like a boy? Jed and I fooled the bounty hunters."

"That was in the dead of night," said the old woman. "This is the cold, hard light of day."

"But how did you know?" Valor insisted.

"You looked familiar. I thought I recognized you. Besides, females has a certain soft way about them. They sit different. They move different. And you ain't got a beard." The old woman chuckled.

"Jed doesn't have a beard yet," said Valor. "How does a boy sit?" she asked.

"A boy sets with his knees wide apart," said Aunt Becky. "Us females been made to set like ladies. Here, now set with your boot slung across your other knee."

"Like this?" asked Valor, trying to remember how Jed sat when he was whittling with Ben.

"More like it," said the old lady. "Now we's got to holp you walk more like a boy. Walk across the floor to me."

Valor tried to walk as Jed did when they went

hunting, his head slung back and his rifle over his shoulder.

"Bigger steps," said the old witch-woman. Valor strode across the room, her arms swinging widely. "Not too big," she chuckled. "Or you'll look like you playing the fool."

Throughout the morning Valor practiced being a boy. When the old woman was satisfied that anyone who saw her move would believe Valor not to be female, she took the girl out to a smokehouse in the backyard.

Opening the door, she invited Valor into the fragrant darkness.

"Here's where I dries my yarbs," the old woman said softly. She led Valor around the room until the girl's eyes grew accustomed to the gloom. "Peach bark tea. Make the measles come. Catnip good for teething babies. Mint soothes the stomach and helps the body use the food you eat." She touched bunches of herbs hanging from the rafters as she spoke. Then she opened a cloth bag hanging in a dark corner. "And this here's my sleeping soother. What's in it is a secret, but it will put a horse to sleep if you put it into his drinking water. Taste's sweet, so's they's no bad taste either."

"What do you use it for?" asked Valor.

"Use it only when a person be real sicklike and need to rest. Or when a person be dying all eat up inside so's they can't get no relief from the agony. Bile it up with some sassafras root and it go down real easy. Only a body ain't hardly got no strength to move. You slip this into a pot of boiling water, it'll make men too weak to move for a day or two. Even filthy renegades."

The old wise-woman lifted the bag down from the nail on the wall, added sassafras roots from a wooden pail, and carried the bag through the door. As they walked back into the kitchen, she set the bag on the table.

"I saw them renegades pass up the road yesterday about sundown. They was headed up the river road toward the Trail. They had some sheep, about six head of cows, four horses, and one pretty little roan filly. That must have been your Sam. Fine name fer a pretty little horse, I'd say." The old lady chuckled. "These yarbs be mighty holpful to what you're aiming to do."

"I sure would like to get her back," said Valor. "So I better get on up the road. Ma'am, I'm much obliged to you for your help."

"Whoa, Little Sister," the old woman laughed her soft laugh. "Valiant. I ferget. You ain't ready to set out just yet."

The old woman stopped to rest.

"I'm fixing you a bag of my sleeping soother. If a lost boy comes wandering into their camp, they'll welcome help with the cooking. You can make them a pot of yarb tea. When they's asleep, you can steal your livestock and your little filly."

Valor began to laugh out loud. She clapped her hands. "Auntie, you are wonderful! My papa said you were the kindest person on earth, and I believe it. You are a sister to the wind. Oh, I hope I can be like you!"

"If'n I was ten years younger, I'd set out with you," sighed the old lady. "But I'm afraid these old lags wouldn't hold out. I can still ride, but I can't walk very far. Anyways, if you can get the cattle back this far, you can hide them in my barn out back. They done stole every animal I had on the place, so they won't bother me again. Besides, they's afraid of me. Some folks thinks I'm a witch-woman. Scares off some folks."

Valor stood looking at the tiny woman with her shining eyes and her topknot and her long white hair. She smiled. Her papa had been right. This was the kindest of women.

"Now, I want you to set out by nightfall," said the old woman. "I'll fix us some supper in a while. Right now, I want you to go into the front room and

175

sleep until supper's ready, so's you'll be rested up.''

Valor waited. Tears sprang to her eyes. Her lip trembled. Now that the time had come to actually hunt the marauders, fear filled the girl's throat, threatening to choke her.

''Auntie, I'm so fearful,'' she said. ''I don't have the courage to do this.''

Valor sat with a thump on the nearest chair. The old lady moved toward her. She put her arms around the girl and pulled Valor's head to her shoulder, soothing her and whispering. ''Courage is not lack of fear, my little one. Courage is feeling great fear, but doing a thing because it must be done.'' She stopped for a moment and led Valor toward the front room. ''By voicing your fear, you have called on the courage that lies within you. Now, you rest until supper's done, my little sister to the wind.''

CHAPTER 18

Clouds covered the moon as Valor made her way out of the old woman's yard, her body warmed by strong herb tea and hot food, and rested by a long nap. She waved toward the gate, where the old woman stood with a lantern held high over her head.

At the foot of Roaring Creek, where the stream met the North Toe River, Valor began the long climb toward the crest of the mountain. As the road grew steeper, she heard the roaring sound as the swiftest creek in the county splashed its way over the high rocks and down the waterfalls. The climb was steep, and Valor stopped often to rest. Her legs ached from the effort of the incline.

Finally, the sky turned pink and then orange. As the sun rose to her back, she topped the crest and began her descent into the narrow valley still shaded by the mountaintop. The road was slick from the night's rain, but as the sky grew lighter, she could make out horseshoe tracks in the narrow bank on either side of the road. She knelt to examine the tracks as she made her way down the road. Finally, she saw what she had been looking for.

Ben had always taken great pride in the horseshoes he made for Papa's horses. Valor searched through the tracks until she found the raised "M" Ben crafted into the frog of every horseshoe he created for John McAimee. The marks meant the McAimee horses and her filly, Sam, were not far ahead. She straightened her aching back and rubbed her neck.

With renewed strength, Valor began to skip down the road. Suddenly, remembering that Jed never skipped, she swaggered over the rocks, kicking mud as she went. After a while, she began to look for a place to rest. She spotted an outcropping of rock high in the meadow above the road. Climbing carefully up the hill, she saw that a dark spot near the bottom of the cliff was a small cave hidden by the overhanging rock.

Valor made her way up the hill to the entrance of the cave, sat down, dropped her haversack beside her, placed the rifle across her knees, and pulled Ben's hat down to shade her eyes. She pulled her knees up to her shoulders. Then she remembered what the old woman had told her. Girls are trained to sit like ladies. Until her mission was accomplished, she could not afford to be a lady, so she stretched her legs out straight in front of her and crossed them at the ankles. She thought that was the way Jed usually sat. Soon she was asleep.

A low rumble, like deep thunder in the distance, woke Valor. Sticks popped. She pushed Ben's hat back and looked up. The sun had grown dark as if a cloud covered it. Then the darkness growled. It had two ears and blocked the light. A large black bear stood upright, his hind legs on a rock above her, a rasping sound coming from its throat. Valor struggled to get to her feet. She grabbed her rifle and took aim with shaking hands.

"Oh, my lordy," she said aloud. "I'll never kill this bear with one shot!" She took aim and fired. The bear recoiled. He was hit, but not fatally.

Dropping the rifle and yanking the pistol from Jed's pants, she grabbed one wrist with the other hand to stop it from shaking as the bear growled again and took a step toward her. He looked as tall as the trees nearby. She looked up again. Ben's hat fell to the ground. The bear snarled at her.

Pulling the trigger, Valor waited for what seemed an eternity for the bear to react. He fell to all four feet and his growl became a guttural scream as he lunged off the rock toward her. He lost his footing and slid down the hill. As he fell backward, Valor could see two red spots on his chest. He regained his footing and began to climb back up the hill toward her. She moved away from the mouth of the cave, and grabbing her haversack with one hand and the rifle with the other, she began to run around the edge of the rock. As she reached the ledge a shot rang out high over her head, and the bear fell backward down the hill.

Shaking, she sat down on the ground. Tears formed in her eyes. Then she remembered the old woman's words. She must remember that she was *not* a girl—at least not until the cattle and Sam were safely home again. She was a sister to the wind. She could do anything she had to do. She bit her lip. She took off Ben's hat and fanned herself with it.

"Hey, there-r-r, ye!" called a voice high above her head. Valor looked up. Standing on a cliff was a young man with a blue Yankee hat pulled down over his eyes. He waved his rifle at Valor. "Hey, lad, be ye safe?"

"Yes," Valor managed to answer. "Is the bear dead?"

The man made his way around the edge of the

cliff and climbed down to where Valor was standing.

"Why, you're just a sapling." The man laughed. His *r*'s sounded strange to Valor's ears. She looked up into the greenest eyes she had ever seen. Her face turned bright red and her body felt warm and flushed. But the man didn't seem to notice. He continued to smile at her. She stared at his beard, almost as black as the bear, and at his straight white teeth with a small gap in the front, a smile lighting up his face under the cap. He was the most hand-some man Valor had ever seen. And he wasn't much older than she was.

"Brave lad," he said. "Taking on a bear-r-r with only the old guns. Good thing I was out here. You would-nae have time to reload that muzzle loader. Next time ye go hunting, take a proper gun, lad." His *r*'s blurred on into his next words. Valor had never heard anyone whose words sounded as if he were singing them. The man reached out and tousled her hair. "You're too young to be out here on the creek alone. Where ye from?"

To Valor's great relief, he didn't wait for an answer but started down the hill, leading his horse through the undergrowth. "Let's see what our bear is like."

Valor picked up Ben's hat and straightened her

shoulders. *"Our* bear," the man had said. Just wait until she told Jed she had helped kill *OUR* bear. She hopped down the hill, trying to contain her joy.

The man turned around. Her face turned red again as she stared into green eyes. He smiled at her and knelt beside the bear.

"Big one, but poor-r-r from his winter's sleep," he said. "Male. He would have been a mean one. Ye must have found his cave. Good thing I was hunting some meat. Sure got plenty here, thanks to ye. What's your name, lad?"

"Val . . . Valiant," stuttered Valor, trying to lower her voice, which kept getting higher each time she spoke.

"Well, Valiant," the man said without looking up. "Ye are well named. Can't many boys your age say they've been on a bear hunt and killed a bear. Your pa will sure be proud of ye. Can ye bring my horse down from the ridge while I figure out how to get this bear back to camp, Valiant?"

"Yes, sir," she said, slinging her haversack across her shoulder and struggling up the side of the cliff. When she returned with the horse, the man had gutted the bear and was stripping willow saplings from the creek bank to tie the bear's paws.

"I'm Laird Randall McKenzie, called 'Randall,' fresh come over from Scotland, but a new citizen of this fair state," the man said. "Happy to make your acquaintance, Valiant." He didn't stop for a breath. "We have to make a drag to haul this bear back to camp. It'll feed the men for a week, I guess. They wanted some fresh meat, but I never counted on this much. You like bear meat, Valiant?"

"Not much," said Valor wrinkling up her nose. Quickly she caught herself. *Would Jed do that?* she asked herself. The man didn't seem to notice as he worked on the bear carcass. She had to remember that she was supposed to be a boy. She had often helped Jed dress the game they killed, and she had watched Ben butcher the hogs. Once she had helped Savannah kill and dress a goose for Christmas dinner.

She knelt beside the man. He turned toward her. "Valiant, will ye . . ." He looked at her as he worked on the bear. She looked at his eyes. They were as green as the first grass that peeped through the snow on the sunny slopes. She stood up and shook her head.

"Valiant, did ye hear what I said?" The man stood beside her. He was much taller than she was. "Be ye all right? Ye look a mite peaked."

"I'm sorry," she said, remembering to lower her voice again. "I was thinking about the bear and what I would have done . . ." Her voice trailed off.

"Pretty big day for a boy your age, I reckon." He laughed. "Facing a bear is a scary thing. But ye were truly valiant. Ye di'nae run. Ye fired that old pistol right in his face. Mayhap it was truly your shot that killed him. Your pa will be so proud of ye. I guess this bear skin rightfully belongs to ye. We'll see what Kirk says about it."

"Kirk?" asked Valor, her stomach turning over as if someone had hit her. She reached up to touch Papa's medal inside her shirt.

"Colonel Kirk. I'm the cook in his main camp. He is out buying cattle from the farmers to sell to the army."

"Which army?" asked Valor.

"The one that pays the best price." Randall laughed. "I don't question. I left Scotland to get away from wars, and here I am in the midst of another one. I am a tinker by trade. I'd rather mend than kill, so I cook and mend instead of fighting."

He took a hatchet from his saddlebags and cut two small trees. Then he trimmed the branches to make two poles. He stuck the poles between the bear's paws from front to back and he tied the bear's paws together. He tied one end of the poles together. Then he stood up.

"Can ye help me lift this carcass? We'll tie these

poles to the saddle of my horse and make a drag."

Valor grabbed one end of the poles. When Randall said, "Lift!" she struggled with her end. With great effort she managed to lift them just slightly off the ground. Randall moved around so that the ends of the poles near the bear's head were tied to the saddle. Leaning the poles against the horse's side, he walked around to arrange Valor's end. With a heave from Randall, the bear's carcass lay across the drag.

"He's pretty heavy," said Randall, "but we don't have far to go." He looked down at Valor again. But she could see nothing but his bright green eyes. "Ye really are just a wee bit of a lad, aren't ye?" Randall continued. "How old will ye be? About eight or nine?"

"I'm ten," Valor said, "but I'm small for my age. My pa says I'll grow. He was small for his age too."

"What are ye doing out here alone?" asked Randall.

"I'm traveling to live with my aunt in Tennessee. My parents are dead," she lied.

"Well, you're in Tennessee now, lad. Where ye be from?"

"Over near Elsie in Mitchell County in North

Carolina,'' said Valor. ''But my family's all dead,'' she repeated.

''Kirk and his men were over there just two days ago,'' said Randall. ''Did you see any of them? They brought some good cattle and one fine little filly. A prime little chestnut. That's a horse I would like to own myself.''

Valor bit her tongue. ''We live out on a farm away from the road. No, I never saw Kirk's men,'' she lied again.

''I thought ye said your family was dead,'' Randall said.

''They are. I been living with neighbors,'' Valor stammered. ''I really need a job so I can get some food. I could help you cook if you would help me restock my bag for my journey. I helped Mrs., ah, Savannah cook sometimes.''

''I could use some help,'' said Randall, puzzling with his beard. ''Come on back to camp with me, and I'll speak to Kirk.''

He picked up the reins. Valor slung her haversack and rifle over her shoulder. She tried to match his stride as they made their way down the mountain, but she had to run to catch up.

''We'll have bear roasted on the spit tonight, I'll vow,'' said Randall. ''With gratitude to my young friend, Valiant.''

Randall slapped an arm across Valor's shoulders and they walked side by side, the man guiding the horse with its burden through the underbrush. Her shoulder felt warm where his hand had touched her.

CHAPTER 19

Randall whistled a tune as they walked down the winding road. Then he began to sing,

"The gypsy rover came over the hill,
And down through the green wood so shady.
He whistled and sang 'til the green wood rang,
And he won the heart of a lady."

Valor was startled to hear the song Papa had sung to her as they rode through the dark woods of the hill farm when she was a child. She smiled as she joined the young man,

"Ah dee do. Ah dee do da day.
Ah dee do, ah dee daisy.
He whistled and sang 'til the green wood rang,
And he won the heart of a lady."

They sang all the verses as they walked along. Valor's heart soared. All the sorrows and fears of recent days seemed to melt as she sang.

"Do ye know this one?" Randall asked her, with a wink.

"Where air ye going, Laird Randall, my son?
Where air ye going, my darlin', my own?"

"Yes, my papa used to sing that to me. He said his ma brought it over from Scotland," said Valor.

"It is a song of the Scots," said Randall. "My mother loved the song and sang it often to me. She loved it so much that my name is from the song, but my own favor-r-rite is 'The Gypsy Rover.' Do ye like that one?" The strange r's sounded again.

"Yes, it was Papa's favorite," said Valor.

"Good. Then, shall we sing it again?" asked Randall.

They sang the song over and over. Then they whistled the tune together as they walked. Suddenly, Randall put his fingers to his lips. "Shhh!" he whispered. Valor could hear shouts and the sound of laughter in the distance.

"I di'nae know we were so close to camp," said Randall. "I'll speak to Kirk and ask him to take ye on as a cook's helper."

"Oh, thank you," she said, her throat growing tight as she faced again seeing the tall, red-bearded man who had destroyed so much that she had always loved.

"Bear!" shouted a soldier cleaning his rifle at the edge of the camp, running over to examine the bear's black fur.

"As poor as Job's turkey. Not much meat on them bones," the soldier said.

"It's meat," said Randall. "Since we can nae butcher any of the cattle, it's all you'll get this day."

A tent flap was pushed back. A man with a long red beard stooped over to emerge into the sunlight. Valor stared at the man. Although he had a red beard, she had never seen him before in her life. "It's a fine hunter you are, for a cook, Laird Randall," the man said.

"I'm afraid it's nae my kill," said Randall, with a wide grin. "The lad here faced this beast with only one old pistol and that old muzzle loader. Even when the bear was wounded, the lad here di'nae run. He stayed and fired."

"Quite a hunter," said the red-bearded man. "And who might you be, young man?"

"I'm . . . I'm . . . Val . . . Valiant McAimee . . . from over near Elsie in Mitchell County," Valor stammered.

"Fine country," said the man. "Some of my men were over there a few days ago. Bought some prime cattle and horses. I'm Colonel George Kirk."

This was *not* the man who had shot Ben and who had hurt her mother so long ago. Valor was confused. She could think of nothing to say, so she stared at him. Red Beard had pretended to be Colonel Kirk. Now she might never find him or the livestock he had stolen.

"Valiant here could use a few meals and some supplies, and I could use a helper," said Randall. "Can we find a place for him, Colonel?"

"I think we could find a place for such a fine bear hunter in Colonel Kirk's forces, don't you, Laird Randall? I suppose your sympathies are with the cause, young man?" the bearded man asked.

"Yes, sir," said Valor quickly, wondering which cause he was talking about. "Yes, sir, my whole family's off fighting somewhere in Virginia."

"Good," said the man, extending his hand. "Welcome to our company. He can share the tent with you, Laird Randall. Best get to work now, boy."

"First we skin this bear, lad," said Randall. Several men gathered around. One began to sharpen his hunting knife on a whetstone, which he then passed around to the others.

"Ye can get some turnips and sweet potatoes from the cook's tent and wash them down in the creek while we cut up the meat," said Randall to Valor.

Valor was careful to place her haversack with its precious cargo of tea next to her rifle in the corner of the big cook's tent as she secured the pistol in the top of her pants. She placed one pistol ball and a tamping stick inside her shirt, and hung the powder horn over her shoulder. Then she filled a basket with turnips. She started toward the door, turned, and looked at the haversack.

I'm safe. Even if they look inside, they will have no idea what the tea is, she thought.

By the time she had washed the vegetables, several men were turning huge pieces of meat on a spit over the fire. Randall wore a dirty shirt tied around his waist as he sliced the turnips and threw them into a huge iron pot. He wiped his hands and began to bury the sweet potatoes in the ashes of the fire.

"Now we'll make some corn pone," he told Valor. They mixed the cornmeal with water and each of the men in camp brought his small black skillet seasoned with salt pork drippings to where Valor stood shaping pillows of the cornmeal mixture into corn pones. She placed one pone in each skillet.

Then the men returned to their smaller campfires to cook them.

Finally, the feast was ready. Randall and one of the larger men moved the meat to a table, where chunks were distributed to each soldier. Valor served the turnips and bits of salt pork while the men dug the sweet potatoes from the ashes with their knives as they returned to their own campfires.

Near the end of the line stood Red Beard, the tall red-bearded man who had pretended to be Colonel Kirk, the man who had caused her family so much pain.

"Where you been, Herbert?" asked the man in line in front of Red Beard. Valor looked up at him. His small hazel eyes so closely set over the bridge of his nose reminded Valor of a pig's eyes, small and mean.

So that's your name, thought Valor. *Now I have a name to go with that awful face. A name for the man who hurt me and my family so much.* She looked at the long narrow face that haunted her dreams. She had never seen it up close before. It terrified her. She grasped her wrist with one hand to keep her hand from shaking.

Red Beard snorted. "Scouting the creek. Found me a farmhouse with a pretty little woman."

"Herbert here might find time for soldiering if he ever gets his fill of women," the man standing behind him said, and he laughed.

"I've done my share," said Red Beard, his voice lowering in anger. "Best raid this month I made. Brought in some fine horses and some fresh beef. Don't down me for doing my part."

Valor wanted to throw the ladle of hot turnips in his face. The best raid that month had been the McAimee farm, of that she was sure.

"I'll hurt you," she whispered under her breath, her hand still shaking. "Herbert Whatever-your-name-is. You destroyed my family." She stared up at him feeling less frightened now that she actually faced the man.

"Boy, stop mumbling and pass me some of them turnips. I ain't waited all day for you to stand there," growled Red Beard. Valor jumped.

Valor reached up with her free hand to touch Papa's medal under her shirt as she ladled the turnips on his plate. She had to remind herself to be brave. And *not* to throw the turnips into Red Beard's face. As he walked away, Valor breathed more freely. Then she straightened her shoulders. She had faced her sworn enemy—and she had been courageous. She had felt fear but she had faced him without so much as flinching. He had never guessed the terror she felt inside.

When everyone else had been fed, Randall filled a plate for Valor, and they sat near the fire. Valor had never liked bear meat when Savannah made it into stew. But the meat roasted over the open fire could hardly have tasted better. Then she remembered that she had not eaten since sunup.

"Reckon ye could get used to camp life, lad?" asked Randall.

"It's not so different from my pa's hunting trips," said Valor. "My cousin Jed and I used to go hunting every time we could get away from Savannah . . ." She stopped. She had almost said too much.

But Randall did not seem to notice. "I never had much stomach for hunting," he said. "In Scotland, most of the hunting land belonged to the lairds, so hunting was a crime. When I came over, I was out of the habit of hunting. I kill for food, but not for sport."

"But I thought you were a lord," said Valor. "That man called you Laird Randall."

"Oh," he laughed. "I told ye my mother named me for the song. My whole name is Laird Randall McKenzie. It's a name, not a title."

They ate in companionable silence. Valor tried not to stare at his face. Her face grew flushed and she looked away. She had never seen Jed's face grow red. She didn't know if Jed ever had his whole body grow warm from looking at someone, but she could take no chances that the man would look at her and see that she was so acutely aware of being a girl.

That night she cleaned both the pistol and the rifle and reloaded them. Randall examined the rifle.

"Fine old gun," he said.

"My grandfather carried it at the Battle of King's Mountain. He was there with Sevier's men," said Valor proudly.

Randall smiled. "Oh, yes, when your people were fighting mine, I'll vow." He chuckled.

Valor blushed. "Oh, yes. I forgot. Your people were our enemies in that war. Now, one of my brothers went with my papa to fight on one side and the other is with my uncle on the other side. It's very strange."

"Lad, killing other humans over territory or for any other reason seems a mite futile," he said. "Seems a waste of life." He stared into the fire. Valor watched him, stealing glances so he would not catch her staring. "But, lad, since when did we humans make sense?" He stood up and straightened. He began to whistle as he went into the tent.

He came back with a fiddle tucked under his chin. He began to play a plaintive tune Valor's mother had sung to her many times.

"Speed, bonny boat, like bird on the wing.
'Onward,' the sailors cry.
Carry the man who's born to be king
Over the sea to Skye."

Valor's voice joined his on the last line.

Randall lowered the fiddle and looked at Valor for a long time. She met his gaze in the firelight.

"Song of the Bonny Prince Charlie," said Randall, looking intently at her.

"I must relieve myself," Valor said, rising and running into the woods. She found a thick clump of rhododendron and carefully hid in the darkness where no one was likely to see her.

When she returned, Randall was playing "The Gypsy Rover" on his fiddle. Someone had joined him with a jaw harp, and a few men sat near the fire singing and listening as the moon rose high in the sky.

"Best sleep now. Long day ahead," Randall told Valor. She entered the tent hesitantly. Randall had pulled off his boots. He began unbuttoning his shirt. Quickly Valor turned away. Mama said a lady never should see a man in his underdrawers. Then she remembered that, until the cattle and Sam were back on the hill farm, she wasn't a lady. She was Valiant McAimee, not Valor.

She turned back and began to loosen her shirt. She did not dare to take it off, but she touched Papa's medal to give her courage.

"You can use that quilt there," said Randall, as he turned out the lantern and walked to the far side of the cook tent.

Valor lay down and listened until she could hear the even rhythm of Randall's breath as he slept. She lay long into the night, afraid to sleep. *Any one of these men would gladly shoot me as one of the enemy if he knew who I was,* she thought. Fear rose into her throat and sent chills through her body. Then she thought, *No, there is one of them who wouldn't hurt me,* and she looked over at the outline of Randall's body and smiled.

I wish he knew I am a girl, she thought. Jed would think she was getting bewitched by this young Scot. No, she had to forget his green eyes and concentrate on the man with the red beard. Somehow, without endangering her plan to get the livestock back, she had to let him know that a member of the McAimee family had repaid him for hurting them.

Finally, she remembered the silk sash with his

initials on it. Savannah had kept it since the night he had hurt her mother. It was stowed in her haversack. She had carried it with her for one purpose. She had her plan. At last, she slept.

CHAPTER 20

All the following day, Valor worked outside the cook tent, helping to fry the sidemeat, making gravy for the morning, and preparing bear stew for midday dinner. She hated helping Savannah in the kitchen on the hill farm, but out here so much was going on that she stopped often to watch the men as they came and went. She was relieved that Red Beard was not in the breakfast line that day.

"Out on another raid," said one man.

"For horses or women?" asked another.

"Herbert may bring back horses, but I'll lay you odds he went out hunting women, not horses," said another.

Valor felt her old anger, and a growing fear of the tall man with long legs and a red beard welled into her throat. But when he failed to appear at midday dinner, she breathed a sigh of relief.

Finally, during the afternoon, she went for a

stroll around the campsite. At the edge of the clearing she found several small corrals. The sheep were near the edge of the woods, and the cattle were closer to the camp. The horses were in the most protected position of all, because they were the most valuable of the animals. As she walked around the fence, she saw the old wise-woman's stallion. Then she saw a small roan filly. Sam raised her head and neighed as she ran to the fence where Valor stood. Valor rubbed her nose.

"Oh, Sam. At last I found you," she whispered. Sam muzzled Valor's cheek as she fed the horse the last of the apples she had brought from home. *I wonder how long I will have to wait to take you away,* she was thinking, when Randall's voice interrupted her daydreams.

"Fine little filly, eh, lad?" he said.

"Y . . . y . . . yes, sir," she stuttered. "My cousin had one that looked a lot like her."

"Could be that the filly is your cousin's horse," he whispered. "I am of the opinion that some of these ruffians are not buying the livestock they bring here. Do you recognize her?"

Valor looked at him for a long time. Her face grew flushed again.

"No," she said at last. "Hers didn't have a white blaze on her face. This isn't my cousin's horse."

"She seems to know ye," said Randall. "She was happy to see ye, but horses are like that, ye know. Certain people they take to right away."

"My papa always said I had a way with horses," said Valor.

"My guess is that ye have a way with all living things," said Randall, laughing, looking intently at her.

They leaned on the fence rail, each stroking one side of Sam's long face. The horse nuzzled Valor's hand and then Randall's black beard.

"She likes you too," said Valor. "Mayhap she is your horse."

"Hardly," said Randall. "I cannot pay for a horse. It took all I could repay in seven years' indentureship for my passage over. When the war is through, I hope to work on a farm somewhere until I can save enough to buy a wee plot of land."

"Maybe you could come to the hill farm and work for Papa or Uncle Joe," said Valor breathlessly. "Now that Ben is dead, he will need some hands."

"Where is the hill farm?" asked Randall. "And I thought your family was dead."

Valor thought quickly. "No, my Papa is alive. He is away at the war. The rest of my family is dead." Hurriedly, Valor described the roads back to the farm, and the view from the house in the gap Papa had built for Mama where you could see the far horizon with all the mountains in the distance.

"Sounds like a heaven at last," said Randall quietly. "Then why are ye going to Tennessee?"

Tears gathering in her eyes, she said, "Oh, I'll only go there until the war is over. Then I'll go back to, uh, Uncle Joe's, to the hill farm."

"Yes," said Randall. They stood for a long time in silence looking across Sam's velvet nose at each other.

"Well, this place won't be our home much longer. Colonel has said that we move out tomorrow at daybreak. We pack up the cook tent after supper tonight. We will head west to Jonesboro, and ye said ye were heading north. Will ye be coming with us?"

Valor jumped when he said "tomorrow at daybreak." Then she calmed herself. She reached up to touch Papa's medal.

"I guess I'll go with you as far as Jonesboro. Mayhap I can get some word of my relatives or ask about the way to their farm there," she answered.

They walked back to the cook tent with Randall whistling softly under his breath. Valor watched him from the corner of her eye. Tomorrow she would never see him again. A lump formed in her throat,

203

and her eyes burned. He glanced down at her. She stopped and looked into the distant meadow.

"I know what I can do for supper. I saw some sallet greens down by the creek . . ." she began, turning her face away from him.

"Branch lettuce," he said. "This early?"

"Yes, and I saw some marsh marigolds too. We could have sallet greens for supper tonight. I could gather some sassafras for tea to drink with it. My neighbor gave me some spicewood and yarbs to take to her relatives. I could use those to sweeten it," she said quickly, grabbing a basket from its hook on the support of the cook tent.

"The men could use a spring tonic," said Randall. "And a mess of greens will do them good. Sure will be good to eat some greens. Yes, go gather your wild things for supper, lad. I'll get the sidemeat fried to season it with. Tea will be a welcome change too."

Valor hurried to the creek bank with a basket to gather the greens. She could hardly believe it had been so easy to convince Randall to allow her to make the tea.

But as she picked the greens, she grew sad. *If Laird Randall drinks the witch-woman's tea, he will go to sleep too. When he wakes up, he will know what I have done. And I will never see him again,* she said to herself.

She set the basket on the ground and stood watching the creek for a while, a weight on her chest that made breathing difficult.

But if I don't, Mama and Jed and Savannah will starve. I have to take the horses and cattle back to the farm, said Valor to herself. *Besides, he thinks I am a boy. I can't go on pretending forever.* So she finished picking the greens, her hands moving slowly as her mind tried to slow the time that was passing so quickly into the night.

As she sat beside the stream, she reached into her shirt and pulled out Papa's medal. Holding it in her hand, she read the words, "For Valor."

"I must remember that my name means 'courage.' I must have courage. Papa counted on me to have courage," she whispered. "And courage means doing what I have to do, Laird Randall or no. I must be a sister to the wind."

She placed her forehead on her arms where they crossed her knees. She held the medal lightly in one hand as silent tears wet the ribbon attached to it.

"Oh, God," she prayed, "please give me the courage to do what I have to do." Finally, she pinned the medal beneath her shirt and picked up the basket of greens.

CHAPTER 21

Word came that General Grant had seized the railroads into Richmond over in Virginia. Shouts echoed through the camp as the news spread.

The men were boisterous at dinner, loudly singing praises for the first greens of the season, served wilted with fried sidemeat and corn pone.

Valor boiled the big coffeepot full of the old witch-woman's herb tea. Its fragrance was much sweeter than the acrid sassafras odor, and the men crowded around for second cups. Valor and Randall would eat when everything was cleaned up from the meal.

As Valor finished packing the pots, she said to Randall, "I'll clean up if you'll play us a tune on your fiddle. Then we can eat."

He brought his fiddle out of the tent. He tucked

it under his chin and began to play a plaintive and lonely tune, as they sat beside the dying fire. Then he lowered the fiddle and plucked the strings. He sang in a deep voice,

> "Over the hills, over the hills,
> Over the mountains,
> Home.
> I come from far over the sea.
> Now I go over the mountains, home.
> Over the hills, over the hills,
> Over the mountains,
> Home."

"That's a pretty song," said Valor. "I never heard it before."

"I made it up," said Randall. "Sometimes I get heartsick for the hills of Scotland, the purple hills of my home. Now I go over the mountains looking for something I've yet to find. The place my heart will call home."

Valor looked at his face. She knew he meant something more than a place, but she couldn't quite know what it was. She turned her face away and looked into the dark woods. Then she folded her arms across her knees and dropped her face to her forearms.

She looked up at the sky and thought, *Dear Lord, please help me get these cows and horses back over the hills, home.*

"Val."

She didn't answer.

"Val." The voice repeated and she startled.

"Val, could I please have some of that tea you made?" Randall's voice said. "I'd like a cup before I start packing."

She picked up the coffeepot and poured two cups of the witch-woman's herb tea. She carried one of them over to where Randall sat, his fiddle on his knee. She stood looking at him, trying to memorize how he looked, the firelight dancing in his green eyes. She wanted to remember how he looked so she would never forget.

Valor reached out the tin cup toward Randall and looked at him again. She hesitated, then handed it to him. She pretended to drink from the other cup.

The men sat around the fire, and one by one they began to doze off. A few made their way back to the tents. Colonel Kirk sat on a stool that leaned against a tree, his head nodding.

When the colonel was snoring softly, she poured another cup of tea and walked to the horse corral where the guard stood duty.

"Night's chilly," she said. "I brought you a bit of yarb tea to ward off the chill."

"Much obliged, boy," the man smiled a toothless smile. Valor smiled back and walked over to rub Sam's nose. Sam neighed softly.

"Fine little . . . filly," said the toothless guard. His tongue was thick and his head had begun to nod. Finally, he sat on the ground, letting his rifle fall beside him.

Valor walked as fast as she could back to the cook tent. Randall lay against a sack of cornmeal, his eyes half closed.

"Val," he said. "We've a need to pack . . . I'm so tired." His voice trailed off. "Val . . ." he repeated as Valor dropped the flap of the tent.

Quickly, she grabbed her rifle and flung the strap of the powder horn over one shoulder. Grabbing the haversack, she lifted the flap of the tent again. "Val, I think we've been . . . I'm so tired."

Valor lifted the rifle to hit him, clenched her teeth, and closed her eyes. She hesitated. Even if he woke and spoiled her plan, she could not hurt Laird Randall. Then he fell forward.

"Oh, Laird Randall, I'm sorry, but I have to help my family," she whispered. She turned him over and knelt down to look at him. She hesitated a moment, then touched his lips with her own. Quickly, she tiptoed through the camp of sleeping men.

As she passed a rhododendron thicket, she stumbled over a man's leg. It was Red Beard, the one called Herbert. The man who had hurt her mother and Jed. The man responsible for Ben's death. The man who had brought so much unhappiness into her life. Now he lay helpless at her feet, sound asleep, snoring loudly.

Looking down at him, she said, "Now I can hurt you like you hurt me and my family." She raised the rifle and aimed. "Now I will hurt *you.*" Sighting down the rifle, she drew a bead on his cheek just below the upper edge of the whiskers. "I will kill you, you filthy man."

She hesitated. "Now, I will hurt *you,*" she repeated. Her anger swelled up from her stomach, choking her. Visions of her mother falling down the stairs, of Ben's lifeless body as it hit the porch, and of the blood from Jed's leg blinded her.

But her finger froze on the trigger.

She had never had any trouble shooting squirrels or other game on hunting trips. Why was her finger frozen?

"Now, I will hurt *you,*" she repeated. But she knew at that moment she could not kill another

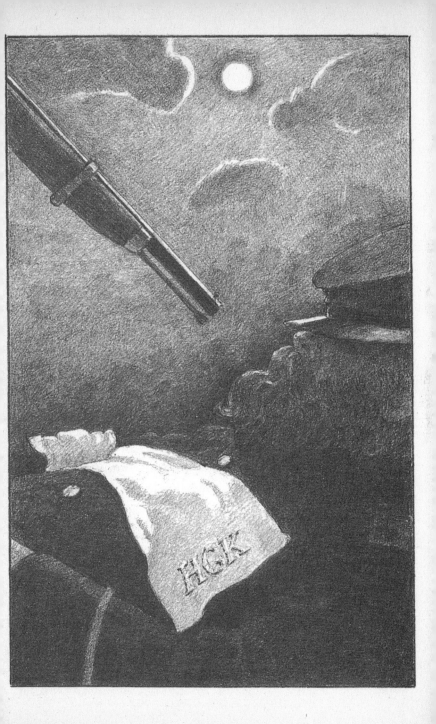

human—no matter how much he had hurt her. She lowered the rifle. She touched Papa's medal. "I'm sorry, Papa, I'm not brave enough to kill this man, even if he has hurt me so," she said, shaking from head to foot.

She stood looking at Red Beard, her rifle dangling beside her. Finally, she removed the sash from the haversack, and lifting his limp arm, tied the sash around it, arranging it so the initials HGK lay on his chest.

"That's for Mama, Savannah, and Ben—and me. So you'll know, you evil man. So you'll know that I had the chance, and that I didn't kill you," she said.

"I'm not evil enough to kill you, Red Beard-Herbert, or whoever you are," she said leaning over him. "But I can give you a powerful headache. I owe you that."

She picked up his shiny rifle and swung the butt against his head, the sound echoing through the trees. She held the gun for a moment, then ran on toward the corral, carrying his rifle with her. She looked around. Every man in the camp was sprawled on the ground.

When she reached the corral, she grabbed a saddle with her free hand and flung it across Sam's back. When the cinch was tight, she held the reins as she opened the gate to free the horses. They jostled one another as they moved through it. "Gee, ha," said Valor. "Get out of here."

At that moment, Valor felt no fear. Too many thoughts of immediate actions crowded her mind. Her only thought was to take the livestock home.

She held on to Sam's bridle as she pushed the horses through the gate. The old wise-woman's gray stallion led the way. The others followed. She threw herself into the saddle and moved Sam around. Some of the horses were already out of sight. "I'll just have to round you up later," she said. "At least these men can't follow me now."

The soldier who had been standing guard stirred in his sleep and moaned. Valor froze, then she leaned down to open the gate for the cows. Even if the noise disturbed the soldiers, the tea had made them unable to stand. No need to worry about being followed. She paused for a moment at the sheep gate.

"They will only slow us down," she decided and guided Sam to push the cows into the road. She leaned down and swatted their sides with the reins.

"Soo, soo, cows," she said. The cows began to run into the darkness. By the time they reached the bend in the road where it began its steep climb up the mountain, Valor had rounded up four cows, the plow horses, and Charlotte. The old wise-woman's stallion had long gone on up the road.

Pushing them as fast as she could, Valor was panting as hard as the cows were when they crossed the mountaintop and started down the other side. She ran them hard all the way to the bottom of the creek where the branch ran into the river.

At last she let them stop to rest and drink from the roaring stream. The moon was setting over the Grassy Ridge Bald. It would be morning soon, but the eastern sky was gray. Her muscles ached and her head had begun to pound from fatigue.

As they made their way down river, the clouds moved in and turned to fog so thick Valor could hardly see. The animals lowed and refused to move faster. They wanted to stop and eat the new grass growing on the riverbank. Then the fog gave way to showers. Soon Valor's clothing was soaked. Her eyes stung from the wind-driven rain. The cattle and horses slowed to a stop. She broke off a sharp branch from a maple tree to prod them to keep moving. "Come on," she said. "We have to get home before the men wake up."

A streak of lightning cracked through the downpour. The cows ran into the woods terrified. Sam bolted, almost throwing Valor into the mud. Grabbing the reins tightly with one hand and the saddle horn with the other, she made her voice heard above the noise of thunder, rain, and cattle hooves.

"Sam! Whoa," she said, pulling on the reins. "Down, girl."

She leaned forward to speak softly to her filly, calming the horse's fears.

Still skittish, Sam danced in circles as Valor guided her into the woods in an attempt to round up the cows. The first cow was standing in a puddle eating leaves. A second was crouched close to an overhanging rock, but the third one hid in a laurel thicket and refused to come out.

Finally, Valor dismounted and broke a hickory switch from a tree branch. She struck the cow with the switch in her free hand as she grasped Sam's reins with the other. The cow pulled away. Valor leaned toward the animal. The cow moved. Valor's feet hit the slippery mud and flew from under her.

The cow bolted and ran off the bank down the road to join the others.

Valor found herself face down in the red mud, her hat gone and her hair plastered to her head. She sat up. Sam was nuzzling her face. She placed her arms around the horse's neck and began to cry. Her tears mixed with the rain that trickled through the mud and off her chin. Sam's nose pushed at the mud on her cheek.

"We did it, Sam," she cried. "Now my family won't starve this winter. We can make the crops, and Savannah can make sweet butter because you and I brought the cows back."

Valor began to laugh and cry at the same time. "Oh, Sam, we must get home soon," she said, lifting herself out of the mud. Her breeches were sodden with mud and water. Her hat was soaked. She threw it across the saddle horn and took Sam's reins, leading the horse back to the road.

Struggling to keep the livestock moving down the road, Valor fought the rain, the wind, and the panic of the animals at each new flash of lightning.

Finally, she could see the dark trim on the porch of the old wise-woman's house. The wind was blowing in gusts. The trees bowed and new leaves fell on her face.

"Aunt Becky," she shouted against the sound of the rain as she rode Sam up to the porch. The front door opened and the tiny old woman came out carrying the lantern.

"Well, honey, you did make it, didn't you? I knew you was headed this way when Gray came galloping into the yard. I was waiting for you." The old woman's face glowed in the lantern light. "Come on around to the barn. We'll hide those animals."

They herded the animals into the barn and leaned on one another against the wind as they staggered to the kitchen door.

"I have yarb tea biling," the old woman said as they entered the warm kitchen. "And they's hot water. We have to get you out of them wet clothes."

"Not the kind of tea I made last night, I hope," shouted Valor, her voice almost lost in the wind. The old woman laughed as she closed the door behind them. She poured water from a pot on the fire into a basin as Valor shed her sodden, mud-laden clothing.

When she was clean, Valor drank her tea. She was exhausted. Her arms and legs felt as if they would fall off. "I'm so tired. I rode all night," she said.

"Tell me all about it." The old woman cackled and rubbed her clawlike hands together in delight. "We fooled 'em. They darsen't follow you back over here now. They'll have to travel on foot."

Valor told her about the bear and the young man named Laird Randall. She told her about Colonel Kirk and the man who wasn't Colonel Kirk, the one who had hurt Savannah.

"Filth. Plain old filth," said the old woman.

"Colonel Kirk was kind to me," said Valor.

"I'm not certain he knows what some of his men are doing."

Then she told of making the tea and leaving the men asleep where they sat. When she stopped talking, the two sat in companionable silence. Finally Valor spoke. "But, Auntie, I wasn't brave enough to kill the man who killed Ben and hurt my family so much." She sighed. "I didn't live up to my name. I couldn't find the courage to do it."

"Killing a man don't have nothing to do with courage," said the old woman. "Sometimes it take more courage to walk away than do another person harm. I think you showed some powerful valor this day, Little One. You was mighty fearful, and you did what had to be done anyway. But you made a fine choice *not* to kill your enemy."

"But I wanted to hurt him. Ever since he hurt my mama, I wanted to hurt him, but I couldn't," said Valor sadly.

The old woman laughed. "I think you hurt him plenty. I vow he'll have a mighty ache in his head when he wakes. You gave him some wallop with your gun. You know that *could* kill a man." She chuckled again. "He asked for that, I'll vow."

"But I should have killed him," argued Valor.

"No, Valor," said the old woman, reaching across the table to take the girl's hand. "No, you

218

should have done exactly what you did. You went to regain your family's stock, and that you did. You be a true sister to the wind, my little one. You gave yourself the freedom, and you found true valor."

"I hope Papa won't be ashamed of me," said Valor sadly.

"Your pappy'll be *so* proud of you," said the old lady. "Almost as proud of you as I be this day."

The old woman smiled at Valor, poured another cup of tea, stirred honey into it and said, "And what of the young Scot, my little Valor?"

Valor felt her face flush. "I didn't want to leave him there. Now I'll never see him again." The tight band of feeling in her throat would not allow the tea to go down. She choked and wanted to cry. The old woman walked over to stand beside Valor and pulled the girl's head to her frail shoulder.

"Now, now, child. You be so tired. You must rest. Your clothes are wet. I have the spare bed all freshened for you."

"No, my clothes are nearly dry. I have to take the horses and one of the cows back to the hill farm," Valor protested. "Then I'll come back for the other cows. I didn't tell Mama or Savannah where I was going. I have to get back home." She began to cry, at first whimpering, then in great gulping sobs.

"At least wait until the rain stops," insisted the old lady.

"I have to go home," insisted Valor, standing to get dressed. "Over the hills, home."

The old witch-woman helped her hitch the horses in a family rope, looping the rope over each of the horses, as they lined up in single file, the cow tied behind the plow horses with Charlotte leading the way. The two women fought the rain and the mud until the animals were ready to travel. Then Valor mounted her pony and led the animals out of the barnyard. As she rode out of sight, the old woman stood on her porch swinging the lantern.

Valor forded the river, now swollen from the rains, and, after riding all day, turned up the road to the hill farm, leading the animals. Shivering from the cold, she fought to hold her sleepy eyes open. Her clothes were sodden. Papa's sweater seemed to weigh a ton on her back. Ben's hat, soaked and limp, hung down into her eyes. No matter how often she pushed it back, it fell down again. Valor had never been so cold, so tired, or so miserable. Her shoulders shivered and her teeth chattered.

"I don't feel like a sister to the wind," she thought. "I just feel tired."

As they plodded through the gap, the sun broke through the clouds overhead. Finally, she could see that the wet earth of the high meadow leading to the house was fresh with grass of spring green. Valor looked at the white house sitting alone in the gap. Shep ran to meet her, barking as he jumped and ran in circles.

"I'm home," she called. "I've come over the hills, home."

Valor's eyes burned from the bright sunlight. She raised her hand to shield them, and suddenly she began to shake. Her hands trembled violently as she guided Sam through the gate in the stone wall.

"Mama. Jed. Savannah," she called with as much energy as she could muster. "I've brought the horses. I've brought the livestock home."

She reached the high front porch and grasped Mama's trellis to help her dismount. She put one foot on the porch as Savannah opened the door.

"Oh, Savannah," she said. "I'm home. I'm home."

"My poor baby. My Miss Valor," said Savannah, stepping forward to catch Valor as she fell.

CHAPTER 22

Valor slept through the long spring days and the new spring nights when the tree frogs sang their songs of awakening life. Savannah and Mama took turns sitting beside her bed when coughing racked her body, which grew thinner every day. Sometimes she tossed and screamed out, the terror of the red-bearded man filling her feverish dreams. Sometimes she swung a rifle butt, which only the eyes behind her closed lids could see, at the red-bearded face appearing in the air no matter where she turned her head. During those bad times, Miss Sarah or Savannah sat beside her, stroking, comforting the thin arms that flailed the air above her.

Sometimes when she was quiet and the terror did not come, Jed hobbled in on his crutches to sit beside the window and read aloud. Weeks passed, but Valor did not hear.

Savannah's onion poultices stopped the coughing, and Valor opened her eyes but she did not seem to see. News came that the war was over. Lee had surrendered at Appomattox. The Confederate government had collapsed. The nation was one again.

Word spread up and down the valleys about Valor's courage in bringing her family's livestock home. Neighbors stopped to inquire of her health. But all Savannah could do was shake her head in sadness. "My poor baby," she would say each time a neighbor stopped.

Jed held Valor's head while Mama spooned warm broth into her mouth. "Each day she swallows a little more. We will keep on feeding her," said Mama.

Then one day as the purple iris in the sideyard lifted their arms toward the summer sun, two men came riding up the hill together. One wore a blue uniform and one a gray. They rode slowly through the gap, then each broke into a gallop. Jed saw them first through the open window. Shep ran to meet them.

"Papa! Uncle John!" he cried. "Aunt Sarah! They've come home."

As John McAimee leaped off his horse to the porch, he caught his wife in his arms. "Sarah. You are well at last!" he shouted.

"A mountain woman does whatever it is she has to do," was all she said, but she stretched to kiss her husband.

Jed hobbled down the steps to meet his father, who clasped his son to his chest and wept from happiness.

Savannah came out on the porch like a tall black shadow. "Lordy! Lordy! This be a blessed day! This be a blessed day."

Each man in turn hugged Savannah. Papa shook hands with his nephew and asked, "Where is Valor? Where is my baby? It's been near four years. She will be a full-growed woman by now."

Sarah took her husband's arm and led him up the stairs to Valor's room. "John, Valor's very sick. She caught pneumonia-fever bringing the horses and cattle home."

"Was that our Valor?" asked Papa. "I heard all about a little girl who followed some renegades from Kirk's band to their camp. Then they say she drugged the men with some kind of yarb tea and turned their horses loose. She left some fellow his sash, that he dropped years ago on her family's farm, tied around his arm so he'd know who did it. I heard it was the little Chambers girl at Altamont. Was that our Valor?"

"Yes," said Mama. "When I think of what might

225

have happened to her, it takes my breath. Seems that you named her right, John. She showed great valor in bringing our livestock home."

Papa stopped at the landing to ask his tiny wife, "How could you let her go out all alone?"

"John, she is *your* daughter, and you know how stubborn she is. We did not know she had gone until the next day. Ben had been killed, and young Jed had been shot. There was nothing we could do except pray," said Mama.

"That's the Lord's truth," said Savannah from the bottom of the stairs. "I'd a gone with her, but she was gone like a thief in the night. And my poor Ben just buried."

"Well, the important thing is that she is safe," said Papa. "Let me go in and see her." Sarah left her husband at the door.

Captain McAimee walked to the bed, looked at his sleeping daughter and turned his head toward the window. He walked across the room to look out so no one could see the tears on his face. Then he turned back to the bed. He picked Valor up in his arms and sat in the rocking chair, holding his daughter and rocking back and forth. Valor slept.

"My little Valor. My valiant little girl," he said. "What has this war done to you?" He continued to rock. Then he began to sing softly,

"The gypsy rover came over the hill,
And down through the green wood so shady.
He whistled and sang 'til the green wood rang,
And he won the heart of a lady."

He stopped singing and began to whistle the melody. Valor moved her head against his chest.

"Papa. Laird Randall," she whispered, but she did not open her eyes.

Papa continued to rock and whistle. "Who is this Randall?" he asked softly.

"Papa," said Valor, opening her eyes and looking up at his gray beard. "I came home," she said weakly.

"Yes, my darling Valor. It's your papa. I'm home," he said.

"I brought the horses home," Valor said weakly. "Now we won't starve. We can plant the crops. But, Papa, I didn't kill that awful man, the man who hurt Mama."

"No, my darling, we won't starve. Thanks to my valiant daughter. And we shall have no more talk of killing. The war is over. Now, how do you feel?" he asked.

"I'm tired, Papa. It was so cold and the road was so long," she whispered. "But I came home. And Aunt Becky says I am a sister to the wind. Do you think I am, Papa?"

227

"That you did, and that you are," said Papa. "My little Valor brought the cattle home. You sleep now. When you wake, I'll feed you some of Savannah's good soup."

He placed his daughter gently on the bed and pulled the covers around her shoulders. Then he bent to kiss her cheek.

"Sleep, my brave little one. No son could have shown more valor than my pretty daughter. Yes, we named you well," Papa said.

He went to the summer kitchen, where Savannah was lifting the dutch oven from the ashes on the hearth. She opened it, and the fragrance of the fresh biscuits filled the room, blending with the smell of chicory from the coffeepot. Mama was lifting side-meat from the pan and adding milk for gravy.

"They's no meat in the smokehouse. Them rascals done turned the hogs loose in the woods and run off with all the chickens," said Savannah. "I had some sidemeat hid out. This is the last of it."

"It will be a feast for a king," said Papa, taking Mama in his arms, turning fork and all. Uncle Joe and Jed came into the kitchen.

"How's Valor?" asked Joe Burl, giving his sister a hug. "She's a young lady of great courage."

"She spoke to me," said Papa. "She knows that she brought the cattle home."

They sat around the table and joined hands. Captain McAimee reached out and included Savannah in the circle as Sarah caught the tall black woman's other hand.

"Oh, Lord," prayed Captain McAimee, "thank you that we be safely home. Please bring my sons home too. Be with the soul of Ben, and please heal my little Valor. Bless this wonderful food and our beautiful home. Amen."

Savannah passed the biscuits and gravy around the table, tears of happiness streaking her face.

Jed told his father and his uncle all he knew about Valor's trip to the soldier's camp to bring the cattle back. The two men shook their heads in amazement at the young girl's courage.

"Good thing we didn't raise her to be a lady, huh, Sarah?" Papa winked at his wife. "Heaven knows you tried hard enough."

Uncle Joe took his sister's hand. "Your daughter has the heart of a lady," he said. "And that of a hero. Valor. She has earned her name."

Sarah smiled at her brother.

Later, Jed slipped up to Valor's room. "Think we could slip out hunting tonight without Savannah catching us?" he said, grinning.

"No. Papa's home at last," said Valor. "And I'm hungry."

CHAPTER 23
(Summer 1865)

The war was finally over. Word had come to the high meadow that President Lincoln had been shot. Both Captain John and Joe Burl were saddened, but the war news seemed so far away to Valor. All that happened seemed to her to have happened to someone else.

The maypops were turning and the honeysuckle was filled with nectar. Soon the tiny wild strawberries in the meadow would be spreading their fragrant goodness.

Valor sat on the porch with Shep at her side and watched as Papa and Uncle Joe brought the four cows across the gap and made their way to the woodshed. The new barn would have to wait until plowing was done so that late crops could be planted if they were to grow before first frost.

"Old Aunt Becky sent some curing yarbs to help

you grow stronger," said Papa, handing a bag to Valor. Tied to the top of the bag was a bouquet of dried flowers and leaves. Their scent held promise of warm summer days ahead.

"We heard the whole story of your cattle drive, Aunt Becky's version," Papa chuckled. "Seems you put a whole company of Tennessee volunteers and a whole army of renegades out of commission for a day or two. Gave some of them a mighty headache too. If Valor had been a soldier, the South might have won the war."

"If we had had Valor, the North would have won a lot sooner." Uncle Joe laughed. "Our Valor is quite a soldier."

"Aunt Becky said that you coldcocked some poor soldier with your rifle who didn't respond to the yarb tea. Valor, what am I to do with a daughter who is such a violent woman?" said Captain McAimee. He laughed as he stroked her cheek, now rosy from good food and fresh air, and growing rosier each moment.

"Red Beard and Laird Randall," she said softly and smiled through a blush. "Randall helped me kill the bear."

"You killed a bear, too? Val, I wish I could have been with you," Jed said, trying to kick the porch pillar with his wounded leg but falling down. He picked himself up. "You got to do everything, and you are just a girl!"

"Young lady, tell me about this bear hunt. That's a part of this story I have yet to hear," said Papa.

So Valor told them all about firing the two shots and having a third one actually fell the animal. "So we took it back to the camp and cooked it for supper. Papa, Laird Randall sang your favorite song all the way."

"What else did you do? Killed the bear, then cooked it for dinner! Lordy, Val. You did all that while I sat here at home nursing my leg," said Jed in disgust. "It isn't fair for a girl to get to do all that. What did you do with the bearskin, Val? You should have brought it back with you."

"It was bring the cattle and horses back, or bring the bearskin," Valor told him impatiently. "We'll go hunting as soon as I get my strength, and I'll kill you another bear!" teased Valor. "I don't know what happened to the bearskin, Cousin. Mayhap Laird Randall took it when he woke up."

"Laird Randall," said Papa. "So that's who he is. And you knocked him out with yarb tea and left him. That's no way for a lady to impress a man, daughter," he teased.

Valor's face fell, and she twisted her hands in her

lap. "Papa, there was another man. I hit him with the rifle."

She was silent. Her father took her hand.

"I should have killed him. I swore I would," she whispered.

"Now, now, my little Vallie," said her father. "It wasn't your place to kill any man. This war was started by men, and our daughters should not have to end it."

"But, Papa, the man with the red beard hurt Mama. He killed Ben and shot Jed. I wanted to kill him, but I couldn't, even when he was lying there so helpless," Valor said.

"You should have killed him when you had the chance," insisted Jed, slamming his fist into the palm of his hand.

Captain Burl clasped his son's shoulder and looked sternly into Jed's eyes. "Son, sometimes it takes more courage to walk away than it does to harm your enemy," he said.

"True," said Captain McAimee. "Better never to have blood on those pretty hands and to have you safe than to have that renegade dead."

"But I tied his precious silk sash with his initials on it to his arm so that he would know that some-body from the McAimee farm had paid him back,"

233

said Valor, smiling. "I hope he thinks Savannah returned his sash. He hurt her and Ben so much."

Her father joined his hands and stretched his tall frame to the ceiling of the porch. "Whatever my daughter did or did *not* do, she possessed the valor of a true soldier, and I'm one proud sire. You have made me as proud as any son and heir could have. You are a true McAimee heir."

He reached down to tousle his daughter's curls, growing into short soft brown ringlets around her face.

"But she has the heart of a lady," said Uncle Joe. "And courage to match any soldier in either army. A man who does not admire both in a woman is not much of a man." He took his niece's hand. "I admire both."

Valor smiled at Uncle Joe. "Auntie Becky says that courage is not lack of fear, but doing a thing because it must be done."

"That's as good a meaning for courage as I've ever heard," said Uncle Joe.

"She is a very wise person," said Papa shaking his head in agreement. "And my pretty daughter certainly gave new meaning to the word."

"I felt fear for certain," said Valor.

"All the more reason to admire my niece's courage," said Uncle Joe.

"Amen to that," said Papa, standing up to stretch. "Who is that coming across the meadow?" asked Papa, shading his eyes. Two figures rode slowly toward them. One wore a gray uniform, and one wore blue.

"My sons," cried Sarah, running down the steps, away from the house through the dooryard, followed by Shep, barking in happy circles.

The two figures dismounted as Valor ran past her mother to leap into Jeff's arms. Her older brother lifted her high into the air. Papa, Uncle Joe, and Jed walked side by side to meet her brothers.

Savannah came around the corner from the summer kitchen, drying her hands on her apron. "Lordy, be!" She raised her arms to the heavens. "My whole family done come home safe. Thank ye, Lord," she prayed.

As the group approached the front porch, Tom reached out with one gray-uniformed arm to hug his little sister.

"Vallie, I like not to have knowed you. You're growed into such a pretty lady," he said.

"Yeah," said Jeff pulling off his blue hat to search for a letter in the headband. "We run into a young feller back at the old wise-woman's house. He gave us a letter for you."

"Laird Randall," whispered Valor.

235

She opened the letter and stood reading as the others made their way to the house.

"My dear Valor. Your bear skin is tanned, and the headache your tea gave me has lessened some. I followed your directions to the hill farm but stopped along the way. I stay for a time with Mrs. Linkerfelt to be of some aid to her in mending her house. She tells me that ye are acquainted with her. She tells me that I might be welcomed in your home if I arrive one day to deliver the bear skin to its rightful owner. She told me of your perilous journey to our camp, and she says a very strange thing to me about ye. She tells me that your great valor has proven ye to be a sister to the wind. Do ye know what that means? I believe it means that I was right about ye all along. I remain your faithful servant, Laird Randall McKenzie."

Valor followed her family to the house and sat on the porch as they talked long into the spring twilight. But she was silent, for she listened to hear someone come riding across the meadow whistling.

"The gypsy rover came over the hill,
And down through the green wood so shady.
He whistled and sang 'til the green wood rang,
And he won the heart of a lady."

AUTHOR'S NOTE

Mountain Valor is based on a true event. Valor was Matilda Houston. As an adolescent, she rescued her family's livestock when marauders took them during the Civil War. Exactly how she completed her mission is not known. The story of this very courageous young woman has been a part of the folklore of Avery County, North Carolina, for four generations, yet no written documentation of the specific sequence of events exists and only one documentation of the girl's identity has been located in ten years of research. Arizona Houston Hughes identified her in *Aunt Zona's Web,* a privately published autobiography of the subject of *My Great-Aunt Arizona* (HarperCollins, 1992).

Valor's role models are also based on real women who lived in the area during the same period. Whether the young woman ever met either or both of them can never be known. Melinda "Sam" Blaylock was a soldier in the Confederate army. She and her husband were among the deserters from both armies who found hiding places in the Appalachian Mountains. They lived in a cabin on Grandfather Mountain during that time. Rebecca Linkerfelt was an herbalist, a wise-woman who was purported to be a witch. Folktales about her are also a part of the local folklore. She is the subject of a picture book, *Heckum Beckum Linkumfelt.*

That one of Valor's brothers fought on either side in the Civil War is not true. The division of the family is symbolic of the rift that tore mountain families apart. That the residents of the McAimee farm seem only mildly committed to either side is also symbolic of the many families whose major goal was survival as they were battered from both sides.

Savannah and Ben are symbolic of the mountain attitudes toward slavery. Small mountain farms used little slave labor, and the early settlers of the Appalachian mountains were too close to their European ancestors' serfdom to be strong supporters of the ownership of other humans.

The language spoken by the characters is an attempt to capture the rapidly disappearing dialectical form of eighteenth-century English spoken by residents of the Appalachian mountains until recent

238

times. Its similarity to black English in some instances reflects a common linguistic heritage.

Many of the words used to enrich the dialogue are spelled phonetically to capture the archaic pronunciations (holp for "help"), which are historically accurate. The speech patterns indigenous to the old Appalachian culture reflect the forms of English carried into that isolated area during the seventeenth and eighteenth centuries. Until the late twentieth century, those speech patterns changed little, but they are now rapidly disappearing.

G.H.